The Daemon at the Casement

—— Or ——

Frankenstein, Part II

The 200-Year Sequel to Mary Shelley's 1818 Classic

M. Reese Kennedy

SUNKEN
GARDENS
PRESS

www.sunkengardenspress.com

Cover and Interior Design: Jason Pearce

Books by M. Reese Kennedy

The Plague of Dreamlessness (2012)

The Artist in the Pines (2014)

The Little Life of Richie Millipede (2017)

The Daemon at the Casement, or Frankenstein, Part II (2018)

AUTHOR'S NOTE

Mary Shelley published *Frankenstein* two hundred years ago (1818) at the astounding age of 20. In her closing pages, the title character lay dead; but his creature's demise, while self-decreed, was unconfirmed. She'd left a fortuitous opening, for we'd seen far too little of her most compelling creation.

Daemon is Shelley's spelling, common at the time, of our modern *Demon*; the two are pronounced and defined identically. The demon here is not the grunting illiterate of the films, but the erudite, sensitive beast of the book. He is not the lurching, slow-footed creature of the many Hollywood renditions, but the agile one who dwells "among the ridges of inaccessible precipices," and "bound(s) over the crevices in the ice."

In any sequel a century or two removed from its original – John Banville's *Mrs Osmond* (*Portrait of a Lady*) and P.D. James' *Death Comes to Pemberley* (*Pride and Prejudice*) are foremost in my mind – the author has some duty to linguistic continuity, or rather, is allowed a measure of its indulgences. Even in describing the most unspeakable behavior, I've aspired to something near Shelley's romantic style, and thus do the paragraphs teem with semicolons and moan with the occasional "alas!" The discerning reader will also note, most likely with some alarm, an early "thitherto."

The question may arise as to the need to read the original. *Daemon* begins precisely where Shelley leaves off, in the sea ice of the far north; but in its course, the essentials of her story should become clear. In a few noted letters she'll tell it herself. But if you haven't already, I'd highly encourage reading the original, if not beforehand, then at some other time. It's a brilliant work, packed with memorable passages; and, if you're pressed for time, *Frankenstein*, compared to the other enduring novels of its time, is marked by its brevity.

M. Reese Kennedy

October, 2018

VOLUME ONE

Chapter I

The cold will always have its way, and nowhere is this more pronounced than at the northern extremes of the globe. I'd persevered well beyond the humanly possible, and the long, frigid chase had taken its deathly toll; I'd lured my creator to his much-deserved end, and paid my own dreadful price along the way. By the time we'd stumbled upon the icebound ship and he'd abandoned his dog-sledge for its comforts, he was well beyond saving. But while he'd lain in that cabin, wrapped in blankets, moaning and sipping broth, I'd suffered a second eternity of cruel exposure – forty days hidden behind a parapet of ice, and forty nights slinking about the ship, unseen by any aboard it. So when at last I beheld him in death, I'd neared my own endpoints. And as I pawed his lifeless form, just as he'd once pawed mine, I grasped what I'd somehow not foreseen, that his death had extinguished the sole object of my own existence. Just as my magnetic compass had spun awry at those latitudes, so now did the inner workings of my person. I left that ship not in a state of true resolution, but of extreme anguish and bewilderment.

You may wonder at my claim to distress over the matter of Frankenstein's death, since every action I'd taken during that time led precisely, purposely, and irrevocably to that outcome. But much as I'd despised him and devoted my every hour to his continuing torment, even as I'd lured him ever northward into the throes of unbearable hardship, he was all I'd ever had. In lieu of a mother, a father, or any forbears whatsoever, he was the lord of my wretched existence, the cruel and heartless master who'd loathed me from the first breath I'd taken, a breath I'd not nor would ever have requested, but had foisted on me at his own ill-begotten command. But even as I groped his icy corpse – he'd be frozen to block within the hour – I recalled the kinder, more considerate Frankenstein, the one who'd joined me long before in my mountain hovel to hear the tale of my miserable life. His attention then would seem but a small forbearance, given that he himself had imposed such a life upon me, and would soon betray his promise to create the companion I so desperately required. But is it truly so perplexing that even one instance of such civilized discourse would etch itself into a heart so despairing as mine?

Some time before, I'd had the charade of another civilized conversation, set in a cozy Swiss cottage on a sunny afternoon in spring. I'd stalked that cottage for weeks, drawn to the warmth and tenderness of the family within. Only with the blind man home alone did I attempt my approach, and my talk with him was the simple deception of the unseeing, short-lived and false. The others returned, and I was beaten with a walking stick; I see that now as well deserved, though my answer then was to burn down the cottage.

The dialogue with Frankenstein in my rain-soaked hovel was altogether more noble, an honest exchange between two seeing and earnest creatures, and the pinnacle of my communion with man, thitherto and beyond. He was well into his ruin by then; that was clear even to one as inexperienced as I in the ways of men. But he held his impeccable posture as the rain beat all around us, and he maintained a mannerly interest and – dare I say it? – a certain solicitude through my lengthy tale, including though it did my snuffing the life from his beloved young brother. Justified or not, the sentiment of the afternoon endures in me. In that window of time he'd shown a true and heartfelt pity. And from what I've seen of this life, to be pitied, truly pitied, is about all any of us, man or beast, can hope to attain.

And so, on the floating sarcophagus of that ship, I repaid my debt of sympathy, though well past any due date of use to either of us. I grieved my creator in death while loathing myself, his odious creation, in life. His demise was irrefutably on my hands, equally so in every measure to those whose throats I'd crushed directly – his aforementioned brother, William; his loyal and affable friend, Clerval; and his fair and gentle bride, Elizabeth. The contemplation of those crimes against him, while in the throes of physical communion with his corpse, inflamed my habitual anguish to a feverish pitch. My discovery just then by the ship's captain, Robert Walton, and his ill-natured assessment of my crimes, further fueled my despair. I resolved then to follow Frankenstein off this earth, to effect my own eradication in the most gruesome manner I could summon, burning myself alive upon the pitiless pyre. In rash pursuit of so harsh a purpose, I harried myself overboard, abandoning that stout wooden ship for the pitiful ice-block from whence I'd come, still tethered, against all odds, by the frail line I'd clamped with a pickaxe.

Having thus leapt, I received my immediate rejoinder, a descent into deathly darkness, a soaking to the knees, and a lashing with frigid spray. The line snapped and the block careened with the force of my recklessly off-center landing. Just that night I'd hauled the sledge from the cover of the parapet, intending to depart upon confirmation of Frankenstein's death; I'd long since released my dogs but had the notion of recovering his, unaware that all but one were dead. Now it was all I could do to preserve that sledge from the clutches of the arctic waters. One of its runners was over the edge, and even during the harrowing exertions of its recovery did I make out the soft splash on the far side of the block, distinct from the general din of the sea; I knew it to be my oar, my only means of propulsion, slipping into the brine. As if to press the point, the wind raked the waves afresh, summoning another wall of spray to strike me like a thousand needles. I dove flat on my chest at the block's far edge, plying the water with both hands in frantic search. It was just then, as I despaired in the frigid darkness, first at finding the oar, and then at replacing it in that land beyond timber, that the flaw in my hastily conceived resolution was revealed, with the sudden clarity that often attends such moments. Any halfwit could see it! Without timber there could be no pyre; and with no pyre, no inferno to consume my miserable frame!

How then would I extinguish life's unwelcome elixir, that which my creator had so regrettably instilled within me? Hurl myself into the icy waters and gulp my lungs full; or lie still on the block and yield feeling by grades, my limbs going to crystal and my last embers to dark, my hideous form lingering then, even in death. They lacked appeal, these passive deaths, this wont of spectacle, these whimpering ends. But with no means of propelling my pitiful craft, I'd no path to a more fitting demise. In a final bitter act, I rose to my feet, bent to my sledge, and cast it with a great roar into the sea, sinking with it all the stores for my survival.

That final decisive deed seemed to chase my angriest demons; I sighed in resignation, spread my single remaining fur across the ice, and lay flat upon it. The night at that hour held no moon, but rather an unworldly drapery of stars, endless in depth and texture, the likes of which I'd not seen in the milder climes. And there, set against its lower edge, was the receding black shape of Walton's ship, bearing the remains of my creator to the south.

Chapter II

Resigned and exhausted though I was, the mercy of sleep would elude me. I drifted off for some part of an hour, but with just one fur beneath me, awoke in a spasm of shivers. The irresolvable chill recalled my first nights on this earth, when I'd suffered in the woods near Ingolstadt, in the scantest of clothing, my ignorance allowing no assurance that the sun would ever rise again. Above this arctic sea, the stars still shone in all their glory, and the gravity of my condition gave them an elevated sway over my soul. The moon had just risen, with what seemed a calming effect on the wind. Water lapped quietly at the edge of my block, and Watson's ship had progressed surprisingly little, an unexpected specter a league or more distant. Silvery undulations resolved as iceblocks like my own; the water was thick with them. If the wind held still, I had a chance for a different end.

I struggled to my feet, labored across my block, and stepped from its far edge onto the near edge of another. I've spent weeks on end traversing the most precipitous alpine terrain, but that was as gingerly a step as I'd ever taken. Repeating the tenuous operation, I moved from that block to the next; and progressed thereupon, as if on some disjointed walkway, bobbing on a pitch-black ether. Exertion returned the life to my limbs and conviction to my movement, and my first stiff lurches gave way to my more customary springing steps. For as long as the blocks aligned favorably, my progress was rapid. But when the gaps exceeded the range of my leap, the loss of the oar cut deep; I could but shiver and shuffle, and implore the blocks closer, as if my own feeble will were capable of shifting the tides. Twice I jumped prematurely, leaving me half on a block and half in the water; only the pickaxe saved me from slipping in for good. Soaked to the waist, I pressed on toward the lantern burning in Walton's cabin, where I loathed him in his smugness and his comfort.

It was some hours before I drew within striking distance of the ship, approaching the side where I'd tethered before. I could see the dim remnant of my broken line in the moonlight, and set myself directly for it. The hull was ten paces distant when I felt the wind renewed and heard its fluff in the sails. The ship groaned and lurched; it would be off at any moment, this time almost certainly forever. No blocks offered further passage. I backed to my block's far edge, took several running steps and hurled myself over the water. I felt my life suspended, saw it in all its cruel folly and cursed it well into my descent, then drove the pick deep into the timber and held on with a desperate determination to live. My body slammed the hull, but my fall was stemmed; I swung thereupon to the dangling remnant of the line and began to hoist myself hand over hand, my boot bottoms tracing their strides up the side of the ship. Just as I reached the taffrail, Walton, roused by the earlier thud of the axe, sprang into view and made as if to resist me; but I was too far advanced and struck him such a blow across the head that he crashed heavily to the deck two body lengths distant. Once aboard I heaved him into his cabin, where he lay splayed and motionless. I followed inside, latched and locked the door, and sank to a seat on his bed.

For all my racing thoughts, and despite my heaving chest and frigid feet, I couldn't help but marvel at the softness beneath me. It astounded me in the way the first sighting of snow or the sea might astound a small child. I, who understood suffering better than all men; I, who'd spent my first nights not in the warmth of a mother's bosom, but alone in the cold, dark wood; I, whose fondest beds were brittle leaves in the gaps of gnarled roots, or sharp-edged hay soiled with the muck of farm beasts, found myself on my first stuffed mattress, designed with the full cleverness of mankind to the sole end of his own perfect repose. Overwhelmed with its promise, and nearly overcome with fatigue, I began to lie flat. But I suddenly reconsidered; loath to spoil the bed-clothes with my wet, rank garments, I stood instead to discard them; and thereupon had a better notion for their use, in the binding and gagging of the motionless but still breathing Walton. Only then, in my hideous nakedness, did I slip between the sheets. The scent there was a bit too suggestive of Walton himself for my liking; but the softness, the smoothness, the ingenious capacity to retain warmth – it was all a wonderful revelation. Bowing to the demands of my unnatural length, I turned on my side and tucked up my legs, whereupon I discovered that rubbing them vigorously against the sheets produced a most welcome heat. I dared not pursue this long, lest the bedding burst to flame.

I remember not what dreams engaged me, but that princely bed, in combination with my accumulated exhaustion and the indelible presence of Frankenstein in the adjoining cabin, seemed to transform the specter of his death into a shroud of peacefulness I'd not known before, in wakefulness or in slumber. In that darkened, slowly rocking cabin, I'd have slept long and deep if not awakened to the unpleasant spectacle of Walton's assault, curiously undertaken without the use of his limbs. He'd somehow pulled himself to his feet and thrown himself atop me with as much violence as he could muster, grunting ineffectually through the gag, which held as firm as his other bindings. I heaved him to the floor, and keeping my hands from his throat only through the most heroic self-restraint – he'd done nothing to endear himself in our brief acquaintance – knelt upon his chest until his face went a deathly purple and his eyes bulged like a toad's.

"Breathe if you will and speak if you must," I said at last, shifting my weight and reaching to remove the gag. "But mark me well; if you dare to call out, that breath is your last."

"For the love of God, get off me," he gasped. When I'd complied, he sat up and wretched.

"That gag is repulsive," he spat. "I don't suppose it was previously employed as a stocking on your odious foot?"

"Yes, for these last many·weeks."

"Only the most vile and despicable beast would employ it thus."

"You forget yourself, sir."

"I forget nothing. I am master of this ship."

"You speak from a position of some disadvantage, bound and floored as you are."

"That may be, but bears not on my legal command."

"I am your master all the same. That welt on your head is as nothing. Know that I can snuff your existence with but one hand on your throat, if and when I fancy."

"I know it all too well," he groaned, and turned away, the very picture of misery. While I'd always had that sort of effect on humankind, it was beginning to bother me less over time.

"I thought you were headed deeper into the northern extremes," he said in half a voice. And then, gathering his courage: "There was talk of your lighting yourself on the pitiless pyre. I must admit I rather liked the notion."

"As it happens, that plan is impractical."

"How so?"

"For the want of timber in these lands."

"We might remedy that for you. We've spare masts aboard, and board lengths for planking. In a pinch, we could smash up a small boat."

"You are too kind by half," I said, standing over him in anger.

"Ugh! Have you no shred of decency? Dress yourself! You are a truly repugnant specimen."

I laughed now, and returned to the comfort of the sheets.

"How dare you defile my bed with your heinous parts?"

"This is perhaps a favorable time to replace the gag?"

"No, please don't do that."

Neither of us spoke for some minutes. Yielding at last to exhaustion, I drifted away from Walton and into foggy contemplation of the deathly trek I'd just managed over frigid waters; of the warmth seeping into my body after untold weeks of such radical chill; of the gentle swaying of the sea; and finally, of the relative merits of life or death after Frankenstein. As to the latter, I found I could no longer assign any advantage to one arrangement over the other, a change in outlook I attribute chiefly to the exotic comforts of that bed. I was very nearly into what promised, once again, to be a heavenly, restorative sleep.

"For the love of God, man, loosen these binds! I can't bear them."

"Do I hear correctly? You address me as *man*, and not as *monster*?"

"Perhaps I do."

"Not as *beast*? Not as *wretch*? Not as *fiend*?"

"As you wish."

"Not as *daemon*?"

He made no final answer, but I credited it nonetheless.

"On such a standing, I would happily remove them."

As I freed him from his bonds, he issued a great string of pathetic moans, and began an awkward manipulation of one limb and then another, as if working them all for the very first time. I couldn't help but recall my own first movements, when I'd staggered off Frankenstein's worktable and lurched about his rooms, terrified and befuddled, abandoned and benumbed. I found myself somewhat moved on Walton's behalf.

"Take a turn on the bed," I offered. I can be really quite magnanimous when not being cursed or beaten. He eyed me in surprise and suspicion, but with an interest I took to be genuine. I held his stare as he came to his resolution.

"That is most kind of you. I'll admit to feeling rather poorly, what with the blow to the head and the effects of the gag. No offense meant to you, sir."

He hobbled to the bed, lay down, and shut his eyes. I wrapped myself in a blanket and sat at the table, which was covered with writing papers. He stole a quick glance at me, which I again met full on; after this he stirred no more. At length, and for want of other occupation, I began to shuffle through the pages.

"That is personal correspondence, addressed to another," he said, without so much as opening an eye. "It is unconscionable for you to read without my express authority."

"Do you now grant it?"

"By no means."

"Who is Mrs Saville?"

"No one of your concern."

I thought of throttling him, but perhaps guessing at my intent, he spoke again. "She is my dear sister, Margaret."

I laboured on for several minutes. I could read a printed book well enough, but my first exposure to the handwritten page made for a painstaking transition, and my progress was slow.

"If you insist on continuing, you may as well turn up the lamp. Yes, that knob there."

"A very clever device. By what fire does it flame?"

"By the oil of the great whales."

"Explain me its workings."

"Perhaps at some other time. My head throbs, and grogginess overcomes me, much as I would resist it. Tell me, am I to awaken with your hands about my throat?"

"If I meant to throttle you, I could just as easily now when you are awake. Sleep if you'd like. Perhaps you'll awake with a better under-standing of the civility within me."

Walton said no more, succumbing to sleep, as he'd later tell me, "against the far greater part of my judgment." I read for most of two hours, gaining proficiency as I went. He'd penned an exceptionally long letter, in several installments over five weeks, the last of which he couldn't have completed more than an hour before my return to the ship. By the time I finished, my exhaustion had become insupportable, like boot heels on the backs of my eyes. My magnanimity had run its course; I awoke him to take my own turn in the bed.

"Do you slaughter me now, daemon?" he cried with a start.

"If one will die of a shaken shoulder, then I suppose I do."

He sat and rubbed his head. I spoke again, partly to calm his nerves.

"It seems your crew has been a disappointment."

"Yes," he said, "they will venture no further. We return even now to Archangel, the wretched Russian port where I hired this ship. The expedition is at its end."

"At some not insubstantial cost to you, I take it."

"To my ruin, sir."

"And yet I presume you have a home, and loved ones – or at least Margaret, apparently – and sufficient wealth to sustain yourself."

"None of that can erase one's humiliation, or restore the honor snatched away by one's treasonous crew."

"The gallant interventions of my creator had but a temporary effect on them."

"He had more courage than they and I combined."

"You are just to credit him so. I am by no means immune to its scourges, but I tolerate the extremes of weather, hot or cold, better than any man. And yet his stubborn resolve, sledging in my pursuit over hundreds of miles of frozen wasteland, unsheltered for weeks on end, disputed that notion. That is, until his final abdication onto this ship."

"He sought you even then. Despite his wretched condition, he refused to board until he'd confirmed our course to be northward, as would abet your further pursuit. Nothing could hinder his avowed task, to slay you for your crimes against him, or to die himself in the trying. I hadn't the heart to admonish him that the latter was the far likelier outcome; and now that I have the full measure of you, I see it was the only possible outcome. He boarded only in the misplaced hope of recovering his strength. And when events beyond my control shifted our course to the south, he undertook to rise from his very deathbed, with the full intent of resuming the pursuit on foot. Failing that, he persisted still, seeking my engagement to succeed his own."

"I take it you had the good sense to decline?" Walton had no immediate answer, and we sat for a moment in silence. "His courage is all the more raised in my esteem," I said at last. "While my endurance exceeds that of all men, my resolve was more than matched by that of Frankenstein, whom I had willfully driven to madness."

"He'd driven himself a good part of the way well before you began your labours."

This remark caught me off guard. "You seem remarkably familiar with our histories."

"Open that chest." Inside it was a thick stack of paper. "There lies Frankenstein's story, and, I suppose, your own. I wrote it faithfully to his telling. He reviewed it himself and dictated what revisions he thought required, as you'll see on the pages. I'm sure you'll find it worthy of your sustained attention." And with that he rolled over and returned to sleep.

Chapter III

I'd have thought myself unfit for even the tiniest chore, such was my fatigue. But Walton's pages, for all intents Frankenstein's own, seemed to absolve me of all corporeal constraints. They were chronicles from the afterworld, the screed of our final judgments. A jug of water thawed over a flame; a nub of bread I'd found wrapped in a cloth; the lamp, table, and chair; these were all I required to read unbroken as the sun rose, grew quickly discouraged, lingered long, dipped away, and rose again. Walton slept all through, excepting a single trip to the chamber pot, the use of which I observed with great interest and duplicated several times over, having previously taken relief only through the cabin window and contorting myself horribly in the process. By the time he awakened I was sick with hunger and fatigue, but I'd finished the entire manuscript.

"I was beginning to wonder if you were ever going to wake up. Perhaps that head injury is more severe than I'd intended."

"I'm quite certain you intended exactly what you delivered."

"Please accept my apologies."

I bowed in the formal manner I'd observed in Frankenstein.

"Have you finished your reading?"

"I have."

"And?"

"I found my own appearances related with tolerable candor."

"Which I imagine bodes well for the accuracy of the whole."

"Would that it were less so. The exact nature of my origin, by way of example, was more demeaning than I'd hoped."

"How so?"

"The obsession with graves and corpses, assembling my person with the fragments of rotting flesh."

"What else did you have in mind?"

"Something a bit more dignified, I suppose."

"Like God creating Adam, with the touch of a finger? Something along those lines?"

"You saw that I'd read the laboratory notes. I had no such impression."

"And yet, reading Milton, *Paradise Lost* and all that, at so young an age, you can't help but take an elevated view." He was completely correct, of course; as I'd told Frankenstein, that was one of only three books I'd had opportunity to read, having stumbled upon it in a mislaid portmanteau along with Plutarch's *Lives* and *The Sorrows of Werter*. I felt the humiliation of both my origin and my ignorance. "Our beginnings are all a good deal more sordid than what's portrayed in the great books," he said kindly. "As, I suppose, are our middles, and our ends."

I contemplated this, in its meaning and its tone.

"Having had no childhood of my own," I said at last, "I was astounded by the account of his. The portrait was so excessively blissful, so beyond anything I ever longed for, or observed in any children I've encountered, that I cannot but think it exceptional."

"My own childhood, I can assure you, was nothing like it. His father seemed a saint, while mine confirmed himself a tyrant and a buffoon, many times over."

"It was all so foreign to me that I didn't even resent him for it. Later, as his torments took shape, I found him more recognizable. And more sympathetic than I might have expected."

"Such generally are men's tales, when told of themselves. And yet, in this case, I credit the telling and more, fully and without reservation. He was possessed of rare greatness, and the humility that doesn't often attend it. I'm honoured to have called him my friend."

"The last one to call him so did not fare well on his account."

"You refer, I presume, to the unfortunate Clerval."

"I do."

He went silent for a moment. "We're going to have to come to some sort of agreement, you and I."

"What sort of agreement?" I asked.

"Order of business. Terms of passage. Lodging arrangements. And most urgently, the procurement of sustenance. I'm famished, and imagine you to be as well. Or does your unnatural tolerance extend to long periods of fasting?"

"I believe I'm rather ordinary in that regard, possibly even disadvantaged. Dangerously ravenous at the moment."

"Then I must see to my own safety and get you fed." He paused here, as if waiting for some kind of response. "That's a bit of humour there. I'm well aware that you don't eat the flesh of men. Except, perhaps, in a pinch." He paused again. "The problem is, I can't just take you as my guest to the galley. The men wouldn't have it; they'd kill us both or die in the attempt."

"I'd expect nothing less."

"You must remain invisible to them, as you've done these many weeks. I'll procure us our meals while you wait here. That, of course, assumes no one witnessed our nasty little exchange at the rail."

"Certainly no one came rushing to your rescue."

"Which tells us nothing, given the fealty of this crew."

"Regardless, you're more likely to return with an armed mob than with a plate of provender."

"I can't fault you on logic. Based on what I know of your experience, you'd be foolish to take anyone at his word. You certainly fared

17

poorly with Frankenstein in that regard. But, with all due respect, and in spite of the rude aspect life has passed to your outlook, you're still quite young in this world – only a few years in, as I understand it. My advice would be to always consider what's in it for the other man. In this case, an angry mob does nothing for either of us."

"How so?"

"I managed to do some very rational thinking in that bed, despite your having knocked me senseless and rudely defiled my sheets. It's obvious I've been an abomination as an explorer. For all my hard-won knowledge in seafaring matters, I inspired such little confidence in my men that they turned against me at the first bit of bad luck. Hence my return to port, my tail firm between my legs. You understand the expression?"

"It seems the customary position for a tail. I imagine it would convey a certain sense of normalcy."

"More like sheepishness, in the vernacular. Embarrassment, defeat, humiliation. And yet I've discovered something as important as a passage through the northern seas, and far more important than what I was more likely to find, an insignificant mountain or some passably scenic bay they might have consented to name for me. I've discovered a remarkable new species, or rather, a frighteningly original rendition of our own. And a quite advanced one at that."

"You refer now to me."

"Correct. But all those pages you've just read, without your personal accompaniment, they're the drivel of a fabulist, just another in the long line of tall tales from men gone mad at sea. I'd be lucky if anyone even agreed to publish the account. And with you dead at the hands of a mob, I wouldn't even have a body to present. Sailors are a superstitious bunch; they'd never abide what's left of you on the ship. They'd have you overboard before you'd gone cold, and I don't have to tell you how quickly that would be at these latitudes. Even if I convinced them to pack you in ice and return you to civilization – and small chance of that given my sorry record of persuasion – you'd never reach a place of science in a suitable condition. Given your makeup, and I mean no offense, I suspect your decomposition would be brisk. And even if you were recognizable as a reasonably coherent body, no one would believe such an anatomical hashwork had ever breathed life. But with you in living form it's a whole different story, a path to everything each of us ever wanted. The book becomes a publishing phenomenon. Frankenstein is recognized for the generational genius he truly was. I earn a bit of notoriety, some grudging respect, recoup my investment and perhaps a bit more. And you! What shall I call you – Franz? – does that suit?"

"No, it does not."

"Give it a chance. You, Franz, become an international sensation, take your hallowed place in the world of science. It's a whole new start."

"How so?"

"Look, you're not without your charms. You're original, you're eloquent, capable, more intelligent than the vast majority of men; and in time, given a stretch of suitable behavior, I might even make a case for your having a reasonable disposition. But your appearance is a problem; you know that, I know that. We'd need some dark glasses – that runny-milk aspect to your eyes is particularly troublesome. You've surprisingly well-shaped teeth, though they want for brushing. A barber and the right tailor could make a big difference. But with your stature and your, please forgive the expression, rather ghoulish overall aspect, you're going to need the right introductions. Otherwise you'll just frighten people, they'll react poorly, you'll get upset, and, if history tells us anything, you'll start killing them. But if they understand your background, it changes everything. Look, you and I are surviving together. I haven't collapsed in horror. You haven't strangled me. We're conversing, exchanging points of view. And why? Because I know your story. I understand who you are, and why you are."

"And on that basis I'm to put my faith in your promise, and wait here quietly while you move freely about the ship, more likely than not to gather your men against me."

"Yes, Franz, I would move freely about my own ship. And again, I would encourage you to consider what's in it for the other man. Frankenstein, upon reflection, knew that creating your mate could make him responsible for a self-propagating subspecies, or master species if you prefer, that could ravage all Europe. And with all due respect, he was probably right. His promise to you was not only personally distasteful, but untenable on a continental scale. And on that basis he was perfectly willing to break it. He held his own life in little regard, and he considered his dear Elizabeth immune from your retribution, or he thought he could somehow protect her, absurd as either line of thinking may appear now. My situation is completely different; my motivations are consistent with my promise. I need you intact. And science needs you intact. Consider your options. Kill me, and my entire crew, as you must do in that case, and you'll founder and expire in turn. Clever and capable as you are, one man cannot sail this ship. But with me you've prospects for a far better life. Here, take this pike. And take this sword. If I betray you, you have your fighting chance. From what I've seen, you'll have more than a fighting chance. Either way, you need to decide. As captain of this ship, I'm long overdue for a turn on deck."

Chapter IV

The battle waged fiercely within me; cumulative, overwhelming fatigue laid siege to my natural vigilance, and resistance grew more painful by the minute. I'd just succumbed to gravity's great pull, gone horizontal on Walton's magical bed, when the cabin door jolted open. I sprung with sword in hand, but it was only Walton, bearing a tray of biscuits and salted beef. When he'd recovered from his fright — some share of the food had gone to floor — he set the tray on the table, and shut and latched the door behind him.

"I thought it was clear in Frankenstein's telling that I don't eat meat," I cried, bitter in disappointment, while we both knelt to retrieve the fallen fare. "Have you no vegetables or fruit? Roots or nuts? Is this what you eat on this ship? No wonder the men are surly and uncooperative."

"You're welcome," he said in an odd tone I now appreciate as ironic. "That pickaxe you left in the hull made quite an impression on them."

"I'd quite forgotten about that."

"They lowered a man down to retrieve it, but it was embedded so deeply he couldn't pull it out. They had to pass him down a bar to pry it free."

"What did you say to them?"

"I played dumb. That, apparently, seemed right in character. But they're all pretty rattled. Unexplained phenomena do not sit well with sailing men. Look at you tucking into those biscuits! I take it the food on my ship is not so bad after all. I'd offer you an ale, or a dram of rum, but somehow I don't think that's a good idea right now."

"I'll not partake in the foolishness of men."

"There's good reason we so enjoy our drink. I imagine you'll take your turn as circumstance allows."

We ate in silence for some time. Just as frozen limbs work slowly back to life, so did my stomach regain its long-forgotten purpose, and my body reap the reward of its labours.

"Nightfall is nearly upon us," he said at last. "And this watch brings grim duty. I've mentioned that the crew will not have a dead man aboard; it's long been a rule of the sea. This night we cast the remains of Frankenstein to the depths."

He'd arranged for our solitude; the men were tucked below decks by nightfall. The body was already sewn into canvas. One arm protruded at a grisly angle. "It couldn't be brought back to bear," he grunted as we bore our burden to the rail. "I regret not placing him in a more dignified position when I had the chance. I left the cabin abruptly in my grief, and by the time I returned he'd gone stiff."

He abandoned his share of the body, which I shifted to one shoulder. While easily enough managed, it was heavier than I'd expected; Walton would later explain that ballasting materials had been added to the bundle. He produced a book from a pocket of his greatcoat and squinted to read in the fading light:

> *Listen, to this secret truth: We shall not all die, but we will all be changed, in a flash, in the twinkling of an eye. For when the last trumpet sounds, the dead will be raised, never to die again. For what is mortal will become what is immortal; what will die will become what cannot. When this takes place, then the scripture will be shown true: 'Death is destroyed; victory is complete.'*

Where then, O death, is your victory? Where then, O death, is your sting?

He closed and pocketed the book. "Corinthians. You may now cast the body."

I lifted my creator high over my head, spun twice, and hurled him several body lengths clear of the ship. After a great splash, and a brief disappearance, he bobbed back into view. The arm rose once, as if pointing to the stars, then rotated slowly into the opposite orientation and plunged, the body gone after it, suddenly and forever to the depths.

"Usually we just slide them quietly off the rail."

"You might have mentioned it."

"And now you must abide by the laws of the sea and join me in tribute."

He produced a pocket-flask and two small glasses, and filled them each. "To Frankenstein, our dearly departed friend and savant," he said, swallowing in one motion. "As brokenhearted as any man who ever trod this earth, but courageous to the end." And then after some pause, "Now you drink yours and repeat, 'To Frankenstein.'"

"To Frankenstein."

The liquor burned my throat and my stomach, but once I recovered from the shock, its warmth was not entirely unpleasant. We stood for some time in quiet contemplation, watching the stars emerge over the swell of the icy waters.

"I've thought long and hard," he said at last. "There's nowhere else to keep you without being discovered. You'll have to stay in my cabin until we've returned to port. Conduct ourselves quietly and we can rightly hope for the best. I'll bring you as much food as you'd like. We've vast stores on this ship, procured at my great personal expense, and most of it for naught. You'll use the chamber pot as required; I'll eagerly grant you the privacy you require. We'll have to work something out with the bedding, fashion you something warm and comfortable on the floor."

This we did, and at long last I slept. While not as appealing as his own bed, mats and blankets on the floor were luxurious by my rough standard, and allowed my legs their full range of length. Walton claimed I was out for more than twenty-four hours. He'd had time and opportunity many times over to muster the men against me, but had proven true to his word. On the strength of that, and on the terms he'd suggested, we settled in for the trip. Quarters were tight; the light was dim and the air hung heavy; we sidled by each other, bore each other's scents. He washed my clothing, and then his own, in cauldrons hot from the galley fire, and that seemed to help. He pressed a toothbrush and a bar of soap upon me, and instructed me in their use. These too were revelations.

I couldn't stand anywhere near straight with the quarterdeck pressing overhead; Walton himself was forced to a slight stoop. But he facilitated my exercise by the most clever means, reserving the regular night watch for himself while bestowing his crew a most welcome run of full nights aswing in their hammocks. This left me free to run about the darkened decks and climb to the moonlit masthead, activities at which I grew quickly adept. With each passing night I more greatly admired the ingenuity of the sailing ship, and could soon execute Walton's commands regarding the positioning of the sails, the hauling of lines, and so forth. In that way the two of us were able to hold the ship's course through nights of moderately challenging seas. Walton's seemingly solitary prowess was the cause of great wonder among the crew as they awoke day after day from undisturbed slumber.

Restricted to the cabin during sunlight hours, I witnessed very few of the proceedings about the ship. Only through my regular conversations with Walton was I able to follow. The northern sea was calmer and the weather more amenable than the crew's long experience in such waters had portended. Favorable winds blew for an unbroken string of eight days, dropped off briefly, and returned for another five. Accordingly, we had little difficulty in our passage. This had a soothing effect on the men well beyond their favorable sleeping schedules. Their mutinous attitudes softened, not to the point of resuming the original exploration, but to a point just short of remorse for their role in its early end. The further south we proceeded, the more solicitous became their demeanor.

Walton took this opportunity to propose an adjustment in our favour. The crew would dock him, and unbeknownst to them, his uncouth and unspeakable companion, in London; then return the ship to Archangel under the command of the lieutenant, whom Walton still deemed a capable and honorable man, despite his rather timid capitulation at the time of the mutinous proceedings. In return, Walton would pay the men the wages they'd forgone with the early termination of the mission, half sterling in advance, and half by bank drafts upon return of the ship. By even the most pessimistic estimates, they'd be home months earlier than if the mission had run any version of its intended course; they'd have sailed through far less treacherous waters; and they'd be wealthier men for their troubles.

Chapter V

And so it was that we shifted our course from the south to the southwest. Walton described the men, whose journey had been considerably lengthened by the terms of the new agreement, as being further cheered; such, apparently, was the sway of sterling. And Walton himself, who conversely had surrendered sterling to shorten his journey, was equally uplifted. "Always consider what's in it for the other man," he reminded me.

In his more expansive new mood, Walton took to spreading his sea charts across our cabin table, explaining their codes and demonstrating the progress of the ship as determined by his calculations with the sextant. As they required a clear view of the horizon, sextant readings were taken by day, and thereby precluded my participation. Accordingly, I focused on the subsequent mathematics, and implored Walton to instruct me in their particulars. As I lacked even the most rudimentary arithmetic, he insisted I begin as would the smallest schoolboy before presuming to any assault on trigonometry.

I applied myself to these elementary concepts with unceasing vigor, partly from my fervent desire for learning, and partly from the absence of other occupations through the long, palely lit hours. Foraging for one's food and scrambling for one's shelter, both of which I'd done from the first day of my existence, require a remarkable portion of one's time and energy. Now these matters were resolved for me. As such, Walton observed that I absorbed as much in a day of eager and unbroken application as the schoolboy might in a year of compulsory lessons. I roared through addition and subtraction, carrying and borrowing with prodigious success; by my fourth day, I was well-immersed in multiplication and division. Walton would leave me a string of problems when he ventured out, and check my work upon his return. He seemed humored by the process; and having on several occasions complimented me on my self-taught reading, he suggested I apply myself now to the art of writing. In that way, just as I advanced into middling concepts of mathematics, I returned to the bottom of another academic ladder, printing with a lead while holding true to a line.

The weeks passed in this quite pleasing fashion. Biscuit and salted beef never advanced in my estimation, but their steady presentation, in conjunction with good sleep and regular exercise, left me in a more robust state than I might have guessed. I could see that the easy life had its benefits. As we continued our fine passage, I enjoyed more comforts, more learning, and more civilized conversation, limited though it was to Walton, than ever I had before. On the wings of this unaccustomed good fortune, our subterfuge held firm; my presence remained undetected. The captain's cabin was the furthermost astern, buffered from the crew's quarters by the hold amidships. The greatest risk lay with our daytime conversations carrying above boards, a risk greatly mitigated by the quarterdeck's double-planking and the regular human commotion occurring upon it, in conjunction with the creak of the masts, the crack of the sails, and the crash of the sea. With regard to my possible detection, Walton seemed more concerned with the volume of food he was hauling to the cabin than with the proliferation of our voices.

Such was my enthusiasm and progress in the studies of writing, trigonometry, and navigation that I rued our approach to London. It was just as I came to the maritime application of the mathematics, just as I stood proudly poised to plot our position, that we entered the mouth of the Thames. In truth, I rued our approach for far graver reasons than the loss of academic validation. The ship had proved a point of safe harbour, and a fertile ground for my learning; and I'd gleaned enough about London to know something of its density, to know full well the difficulties of remaining concealed in such a place, and the numbers that the breach of such concealment would quickly muster against me. Walton understood all of this perfectly well, and calmed me as best he could, while revealing very little of his plan.

A morning arrival would have rendered our stealthy disembarkation nearly impossible; but Walton had scheduled cleverly enough to put us at the docks near sunset. At the moment of the ship's securing, the crew dispersed for a night of long-awaited, sterling-fueled revelry; in consequence, she was virtually unmanned when Walton and I took our turn down the ramp and "found our land legs," as he put it, under the dim lights of the harbour. Our destination was Walton's own residence, a walk of quite some distance from the docks. I carried nothing but the pickaxe I'd recovered and tucked in my belt on my way off the ship. I hoped to gain some measure of anonymity by cloaking myself – far too heavily on such an unseasonably warm autumn's night – and by adopting the most stooped walk I could manage. As we progressed to the teeming core of the city, the likes of which I'd neither seen nor imagined, this combination caused the sweat to pour off my body, a situation so unpleasant that I soon longed beyond reason for a return to the far north, or to the winter forests of Ingolstadt.

Aware of my discomfort, Walton, when not consumed at steering us away from the larger pockets of the nighttime population, endeavoured to boost my spirits, or at least to engage them, by expounding on some the city's great wonders. He sensed my awe at the foot of the great churches whose carven stone thrust so high into the night, and assured me my reaction was consistent with their makers' intent. Between constant exhortations for me to stay low in my gait, or to halt and duck away, he described the superstitions that had spawned those churches; and their puzzling hold on the society of modern men; and the great folly, and cruelty, often arising in their wake. He described the crusades, in which whole armies of men sailed and marched to slaughter distant peoples unprovoked; and the inquisition, in which freethinking men were stifled through incarceration, torture, and immolation. None of this came as a surprise to me, given what I'd seen of men; I was more concerned that Walton could carry on longer than I could maintain the proper stoop in my gait. As my tolerance waned, so too did my stature increase, until, in my exhaustion, still hours before dawn, I stood at something near my true eight feet. With an impressive knowledge of the city, Walton steered us by way of its darkest and narrowest streets, but even this could not prevent some measure of attention.

"Look at the fookin giant!"

"Drunks," whispered Walton. "Stoop and move."

"A right ugly one at that." A bottle bounced hard off my back.

"Pay your respects, monster. Mind us when we speak to you."

"Keep moving," Walton repeated.

I sensed the footsteps and braced for a blow. Instead, I felt my cloak ripped away. I turned to face them; they were five, but bore no visible arms. No poles, no axes, no clubs, no muskets.

"Fookin ugly brute," said one, as another slipped behind and gave me a shove. They flanked me on all sides, a situation which, clubs or no, displeased me greatly. One of them struck me, close-fisted, flush on the chin. I stood now to full height; relieved of the stoop, I felt the strength return to my legs; and relieved of the cloak, my hands and arms were free for my bidding. I sprung to the one who'd struck me, clutched him with one hand on the throat and the other between his legs, and lifted him overhead, as I'd done on the ship with the body of my creator. As before, I spun in two quick rotations. This had the effect of blurring my vision, but my hearing grew sharper in response; I discerned the whimper of the man as my hands crushed his soft bits; and the cries of his mates, and of Walton.

When casting my creator I'd sought only clearance, willing him wide of the ship's wake. Now I strove for maximum velocity over a short distance. It was just under a body length to the near wall of rough-cut stone as I released the man with all the strength within me. He struck in a horizontal aspect, with an expiration of breath and a muffled crack, or several muffled cracks compressed into one short moment, then dropped nine feet to the brick pathway, bounced ever so slightly, and was still. In the lamplight I noticed the awkward positioning of his head with respect to his shoulders, and the dark pool spreading beneath it.

One of his mates now brandished a blade; I skipped just beyond its range, drew my pickaxe and drove it through the top of his skull, surprised at the soft sound of it and the ease of its penetration after long use in the more obstinate northern ice. The others fell back. Walton snatched back the cloak and yanked me away and off down the street. He was in a full sprint; I loped at his pace, one step to his three. We slipped around one corner, then two more, before he stopped and bade me cover myself once again.

"I was trying to avoid carriages, but at this point we're going to need one," he panted. "Wait here, and when I call you out, cover your face and do your best to look somewhat less gigantic."

The night was deep, the streetlamps like beacons, with ample cover in the darkness beyond their reach. I waited as instructed until Walton arrived in a closed carriage drawn by a pair of stout horses whose hooves rang out like a dozen axes. "Ah, Uncle Franz, there you are," he gushed for the benefit of the driver, taking my arm and guiding me inside. Beyond an indignant snort from one of the horses, and the first drops of an autumn downpour, nothing seemed particularly awry.

Chapter VI

While the comforts of Walton's ship had been a pleasant shock, those of his home were beyond my imagination. After our many weeks on a rolling ship, his floors held firm and level. The rains had set in, but well-sealed walls and well-stoked fires kept us dry and warm. The ceilings in every room could comfortably accommodate my height; after weeks of stooping in the ship's cabin, and a long night stooping through the streets of London, it was a joy to stand full and to walk in my natural form. Plush floor rugs abounded; I would happily have slept on any of them had not Walton most kindly assigned me a fully appointed sleeping chamber, one of four in the house. The bed was too short – he assured me this would be the case with any I was bound to encounter – but he loosened the sheets in such a manner that my feet could protrude unhindered with my legs outstretched. An ornamental ewer stood gracefully at the bedstand; I filled it at the pump and poured from it into the washbasin to facilitate the brushing of teeth and the washing of face, practices from the ship I meant to uphold on land.

"Normally there'd be a valet to keep that filled for you," said Walton. "But you'll understand that I released my entire staff in advance of the expedition, having assumed, quite reasonably, that it would extend rather longer. And I can hardly re-engage them now if we're to maintain your low profile."

"I can assure you I'm more than happy to fill my own ewer. As to my profile, I must defer to you."

"Snapping that drunkard's neck didn't help, but I suppose it couldn't be avoided. Nor could the braining of the other, though I do wish you'd retrieved the implement. The last time you left it implanted caused me a bit of difficulty, as you may recall."

"I do regret the loss of my pickaxe."

"You understand why I had the carriage drop us at such a distance from here?"

"You were discouraging tracking."

"And why we must keep the curtains sealed tight?"

Drawn upon his departure, they proved a prescient arrangement upon return. Thick, purplish velvet blanketed every window of every room, admitting no view in or out, and, as I'd later find, no distinction between night and day. Walton lit a number of oil lamps and hurried back out. "Make yourself comfortable, and for God's sake don't leave the house." I dared not insert myself into rooms Walton had not opened to me, and dared not soil the rugs or furnishings, all of which were a marvel to me, in the rooms he had; so I lay on the wood floor near the door but did not sleep. Presently Walton returned with a cart full of victuals, the likes of which I'd never seen. I was particularly gratified that much of it aligned with my own taste, as manifested in a medley of root vegetables – carrots, turnips, parsnips, potatoes, onions – along with apples, pears, and a large assortment of nuts. We sat immediately, and partook immoderately, Walton gorging himself on bread and butter and the whole of a roasted chicken.

"Is the food always so plentiful in London?"

He chewed and swallowed before answering, a custom I resolved to adopt for myself. "Only to those with means," he said with some significance. "Normally, by the way, my meals would be cooked and served by my currently non-existent staff. It's just as well you prefer your vegetables raw."

"I've no experience otherwise."

We said nothing more until some time later, when, stunned with the volume of our respective intakes, we retired to the parlour. We each splayed on our own fully upholstered couch, Walton at full length and I, taking his lead, with legs draped over the far arm. Bookshelves lined the room, each of them stuffed with fine leatherbound volumes.

"You'll do well to continue your education here. But first we need to clean ourselves up. If I hadn't been so hungry I'd have drawn the bath already."

He filled several large pots with water, and at his instruction I hung them over the fire. He bade me undress, which I did with a certain reserve, dropping the ill-fitting rags in a pitiful pile that, to my great surprise, he tossed directly into the flames. I'd bathed in the occasional pond during the warm seasons, but never had I luxuriated so, or achieved such cleanliness as I did now with a scrub brush, soap, and the heat of the water. Walton kindly maintained the latter by pouring supplementary hot pots. I wrapped myself afterwards in a plush robe with a sash about the waist. I have very little judgment in such matters, but by Walton's reaction, my appearance had a certain humorous aspect. We drained and cleaned the tub, and when he took his bath in turn, I was mindful of reciprocating his favor, heating, toting, and pouring the supplementary buckets.

For all the luxury in that house, it was the full-length bedroom mirror I found most compelling. I'd seen a good bit of myself before, more than I wished certainly, on the rippled surface of ponds. But now, with the clarity undiminished and the aspect full, and my person newly bathed, I found myself drawn in for a fresh look. The mirror, in its isolation, forgave my enormity as standing amongst other men would not. While my overall form was not proportioned in what I understood to be the classic form, certain elements were not altogether displeasing; my shoulders were broad and powerful; my abdominals taut and well-defined; and my legs, while amply muscled, were pleasingly contoured for agility and speed. But my appendage dwarfed what I'd seen of Walton's; I feared it bordered on the grotesque. And even so soon after bathing, my flesh, with its intrinsic desiccation, evoked a sort of dusty undoing; and its application formed a hideous quilt, doubling upon itself in uneven ridges where affixed in overabundance, and stretching taut where just lacking. Walton was on the mark; the right clothing would make a great difference. As to my countenance, he was equally insightful; my creator had provided me with an inoffensive set of teeth, but had failed dismally about the eyes. While sufficient in the matter of sight, they lacked a defining pigment; irises the color of thin porridge blended abhorrently with the sclera. I lacked any trace of lashes or brows. And my lower lids drooped in the most ghastly manner, collecting a milky ooze that required wiping ten or twelve times an hour.

While the curtained windows revealed nothing as to the passing of days, Walton, through application of the parlor's great standing clock, imposed a certain daily regimen. I spent hours admiring the mechanical intricacy and the fine finishes of that clock – for all of man's ignorant brutishness, he demonstrates a god-like prowess in such things – and I assumed personal responsibility for its winding, pulling certain chains to raise corresponding weights. As if its physical prominence and the insistence of its chimes weren't reason enough, practical application demanded that I master the formal calibration of time. We took our meals promptly at 7:00, 1:00, and 7:00, and retired to our sleeping quarters just as promptly at 11:00.

Walton occupied himself primarily in preparing the manuscript for publication. He'd anchor himself at his favorite table, its feet carved like those of lions, with stacks of paper all about him, and sigh and scribble and flip pages five hours uninterrupted. After the midday meal, he'd settle back and do it again. I was happy to accompany him there in the parlour, keeping a quiet and respectful distance while making full use of the magnificent library; and I believe my presence may have been of some small value to him. "So much negativity," he might say. "How am I supposed to generate any kind of enthusiasm when Frankenstein himself is so consistently dour?" I would simply nod in encouragement, and often he'd settle back into stretches of productivity. Or he might break on certain afternoons for the purpose of directing me in my readings, pointing me to certain volumes while expressing great excitement at their remembrance; or for the purpose of instructing me directly. While his mathematical knowledge ended with trigonometry, at which I was now nearly his equal, he remained eager to improve my writing, assigning me short pieces summarizing a chapter I'd just read or describing some household object. "When you're ready, we can move along to correspondence. I'm sure Margaret would be happy to have a letter; I myself have been a most unreliable correspondent."

"And yet you have a long letter for her, still unposted."

"You mean the one you were rude enough to read on the ship," he laughed. It lay on a small table across the room, untouched since our arrival. "It seems a bit hysterical upon reflection. You must agree it wants rewriting."

Chapter VII

I became steadily more adept in the ways of domestic life. Experienced as I was at building fires, doing so indoors, with dry stores in windless conditions, was but child's play. More challenging were the other intricacies of the kitchen; the storage and handling of various foodstuffs, the basics of food preparation and cooking; cleaning and the orderly storage of crockery and glassware. Walton, no expert himself, instructed me as best he could, and I made certain deductions as needed; soon I was handling those operations entirely on my own. Bustling about in my robe and waistband, which I laundered daily in conjunction with my baths, I'd have the morning meal awaiting his first appearance, and the midday and evening meals in prompt conjunction with the assigned chimes of the clock.

Our mealtime conversations were of two types: light banter, whereby Walton would endeavor to develop my humorous facilities, with but moderate success; and instructional sessions, whereby he'd draw me out on my reading and expound as best he could on the topics therein; or, at my request, explain something simple – a water pump, a fireplace, a musket – and rapidly evolve toward larger concepts – the structure of commerce; theology; the workings of European society; principles of agriculture, architecture, government, and warfare. So many things I'd seen only in glimpses came rushing into focus. The effect was to make the world seem less foreign and more engaging, less inscrutable and slightly less hostile.

To Walton's dismay, the London papers had lengthy accounts of the incident in the laneway, with special emphasis on the unnatural stature of the murderer, and on the pickaxe he'd buried so deeply in the skull. Accordingly, he thought it best we take some time before attempting to market the manuscript. This eliminated any urgency he may otherwise have felt, and gave him ample opportunity to work the text into its most advantageous form. Whole chunks of it now littered the floor, its pages overwhelmed with cross hatches and lengthy revisions scribbled in the margins. It fell to me to write out fresh, legible copies; this greatly reduced my time in pursuit of Shakespeare and Newton, whom Walton had presented as the true masters in their fields, though well beyond my current station, and to whom I could only aspire to satisfactorily comprehend after many years of application. But the long hours in clerical support of Walton were greatly beneficial to the dexterity of my writing. On occasion I'd call his attention to an obvious grammatical error or a minor narrative inconsistency, and at his bidding I began making those corrections without the mutual bother of his approval.

Walton at this time became active in the improvement of my physical appearance. He instructed me in the art of trimming one's nails, no simple undertaking, as he put it, for one bearing "the claws of a badger." I had no beard, but rather "the cheeks of a lady, albeit a gigantic and quite ancient one"; he did, however, have me sit for a haircut, propounding, through strings of barely audible obscenities and the laboured snipping of his scissors, that while he had no particular training in the ways of barbering, "How hard could it be?" He also took careful measurements of certain parts of my body – neck, shoulders, arms, and more awkwardly, waist and "inseam" – and, upon his return from the next day's errands, reported a trip to the haberdasher, where he'd ordered me a collection of linens, suits, and shirts. "I claimed to be with the theatre," he said. "There's no other explanation for the sizes in question." Encouraged with that little piece of ingenuity, he followed the next day with more measurements and with trips to the hatter and the bootmaker.

I'll confess to waiting quite anxiously for the fruits of those labours. The ill-fitting clothes I'd first taken from Frankenstein's rooms, while supplemented with the occasional pilfered addition, had been reduced to rags long before Walton had assigned them to the fire. According to Walton, Frankenstein had made a sufficient mess of me without "the augmentation of sartorial sin." While we waited for the new wardrobe, he secured me a pair of tinted lenses. I hadn't been measured for these, which left the earpieces too short and the nosepiece too narrow; and given the general darkness of the tightly curtained house, I could see almost nothing when wearing them. And yet, from what I could make out in the well-lit mirror, those glasses, in conjunction with even the most desultory haircut, had a lessening effect on the horrors of my countenance.

Those errands were a more welcome diversion for Walton than they'd have been a week earlier; for the longer he'd spent on the manuscript, the more dissatisfied he'd become. He spent two whole days writing an introduction, borrowing heavily from his long letter to Margaret. He then, at long last, posted the early installments of that letter, those from the 5th through the 19th of August, which included his ship's entrapment in the ice, his first brief sighting of my own person, and the first two weeks of his hosting Frankenstein on the stranded ship. The remaining installments he treated much like the manuscript, filling the pages with cross hatches and revisions, and with certain passages from the manuscript itself, and passing them to me for recopying. In that way I could see the evolution of his narrative in a more concise and revealing format than I'd been able to discern from his alterations to the larger manuscript.

To Mrs Saville

November 3rd, 17—

My Dear Sister:

I trust you are by now in possession of my correspondence through the 19th of August. A letter so dated, and posted but recently from London, suggests its passage at the courtesy of another vessel we had the rare fortune to encounter in the uncharted waters of the far north. But the truth is altogether more pedestrian; I posted the letter by my own person, both feet firmly planted in the City of London. Only now am I at liberty to explain, though the glare of the larger tale will quickly eclipse any interest you may have in the physical journey of its pages.

The admirable stranger we recovered from the ice fragment — Frankenstein, he allowed, was his name — shared with me, as promised, the fantastical story of his life. The telling occurred in several sessions over several days, and was delivered with the greatest difficulty, owing both to his grave physical condition and the horrors inherent in the tale. I recognized at once the extraordinary nature of the narrative, and committed myself to committing each session to paper immediately upon its conclusion, while my memory was most fresh. The wisdom of this approach was borne out as the story progressed and its scientific significance became more apparent. Frankenstein himself reviewed these notes upon their completion, and took it upon himself to correct and augment them as required.

The full story is a long one and cannot possibly be included within a letter, as I'd originally intended. I cannot spare my own pages, nor risk them to the post; and as they number in the many hundreds, a full week's tedium would be required in writing you a copy. But you'll see it soon enough, I dare say in a handsome leatherbound edition. I feared for a time that I hadn't enough paper aboard the ship; those pages I'd meant to fill with observations and illustrations of natural wonders, I found myself filling with what others would likely view as ravings of a madman, or, at best, the hallucinations of a solitary and disori- wanderer. But I have already written to you of the intelligence so evident ·ech, and of the noble nature so readily discerned in his character. In our short time together I'd begun to love him as a brother. You, Margaret, would have taken him to heart, just as I did. And as fantastical as was his tale, I had enough preliminary evidence to suspend the normal disbelief, and enough subsequently to vanquish all doubt.

Frankenstein, from an early age, displayed the most prodigious talents in the sciences. As he freely admitted, however, his youthful interests tended to the discredited pursuits of the alchemists — Cornelius Agrippa, Paracelsus, Albertus Magnus, and the like — who concerned themselves with the transmutation of metals and the search for the elixir of life. As he reached the age for a formalized education abroad, his professors at the university of Ingolstadt, as could be expected, dismissed such pursuits as ancient and useless drivel, and imposed a rigorous turn to the more modern pursuits, those branches of science appertaining to natural philosophy. These appeared to him as overly mundane; he rued "the annihilation of those visions on which my interest in science was chiefly founded," and having "to exchange chimeras of boundless grandeur for realities of little worth." But he rose through the academic ranks nonetheless, excelling particularly in the areas of chemistry and physiology. "My application was at first fluctuating and uncertain; it gained strength as I proceeded, and soon became so ardent and eager, that the stars often disappeared in the lift of morning whilst I was yet engaged in my laboratory. As I applied so closely, it may be easily conceived that my progress was rapid. My ardour was indeed the astonishment of the students, and my proficiency that of the masters."*

"One of the phenomena which had peculiarly attracted my attention was the structure of the human frame, and, indeed, any animal endued with life. Whence, I often asked myself, did the principle of life proceed?" So deeply did his next words strike me that they still sounded in my head hours after their utterance: "It was a bold question, and one which has ever been considered as a mystery; yet with how many things are we upon the brink of becoming acquainted, if cowardice or carelessness did not restrain our enquiries."

---

* Author's note: The quoted portions of this letter, and much of the letter that opens the following chapter, are taken directly from Mary Shelley's text. For more detailed attribution, please refer to the Appendix.

It was two days before he could rouse himself to continue the tale, such were the ravages of his fever, and, I surmised, his reluctance to continue. Much was lost to my ear, woefully unscientific in relation to his own; but it seemed that to understand the elixir of life one needed first to understand its extinguishment. "I was led to examine the cause and progress of (bodily) decay, and forced to spend days and nights in vaults and charnel-houses. My attention was fixed upon every object the most insupportable to the delicacy of human feelings. I saw how the fine form of man was degraded and wasted; I beheld the corruption of death succeed to the blooming cheek of life; I saw how the worm inherited the wonders of the eye and brain. I paused, examining and analyzing all the minutiae of causation, as exemplified in the change from life to death, and death to life."

His pursuit of nature's secrets was relentless, at the expense of exercise, sunlight, nourishment, and proper rest, and of all the discourse fundamental to the human condition. This unnatural negation extended over the course of many months, to the great degradation of his health and of his previously sanguine outlook. And then, my dear sister, came that part of the narrative which I anticipated in equal measures of excitement and dread:

"From the midst of this darkness a sudden light broke in upon me — a light so brilliant and wondrous, yet so simple, that while I became dizzy with the immensity of the prospect which it illustrated, I was surprised, that among so many men of genius who had directed their enquiries towards the same science, I alone should be reserved to discover so astonishing a secret. Some miracle might have produced it, yet the stages of the discovery were distinct and probable. After incredible labour and fatigue, I succeeded in discovering the cause of generation and life; nay, more, I became myself capable of bestowing animation upon lifeless matter."

Imagine, Margaret, the significance, and the weight, of such a moment!

"When I found so astonishing a power placed within my hands, I hesitated a long time concerning the manner in which I should employ it. Although I possessed the capacity of bestowing animation, yet to prepare a frame for the reception of it, with all its intricacies of fibres, muscles, and veins, still remained a work of inconceivable difficulty and labour. I doubted at first whether I should

attempt the creation of a being like myself, or one of simpler organization; but my imagination was too much exalted by my first success to permit me to doubt of my ability to give life to an animal as complex and wonderful as man. The materials within my command hardly appeared adequate to so arduous an undertaking; but I doubted not that I should ultimately succeed. As the minuteness of the parts formed a great hindrance to my speed, I resolved contrary to my first intention, to make the being of a gigantic stature; that is to say, about eight feet in height, and proportionally large.

"Who shall conceive the horrors of my secret toil as I dabbled among the unhallowed damps of the grave or tortured the living animal to animate the lifeless clay? I collected bones from charnel-houses and disturbed, with profane fingers, the tremendous secrets of the human frame. The dissecting room and the slaughter-house furnished many of my materials; and often did my human nature turn with loathing from my occupation. Every night I was oppressed by a slow fever, and I became nervous to a most painful degree; the fall of a leaf startled me, and I shunned my fellow-creatures as if I had been guilty of a crime. Sometimes I grew alarmed at the wreck I perceived that I had become; the energy of my purpose alone sustained me: my labours would soon end, and I believed that exercise and amusement would then drive away incipient disease; and I promised myself both of these when my creation should be complete."

You, my dear sister, can certainly guess at the result of these labours. I've already described our sighting of the gargantuan man-figure guiding the first dog-sledge. If that and the chilling delivery of the tale are not enough to confirm its veracity, you'll find more to assure it in tomorrow's letter. I rush this off to make the post, but first I must have your pledge of silence. No one — and in particular your meddlesome husband! — must know of any part of this until a time I judge more favourable than the immediate present. Heaven bless us all.

Your affectionate brother,

Robert Walton

Chapter VIII

To Mrs Saville

November 4th, 17—

My Dear Sister:

The first week of September found our ship still surrounded by mountains of ice, still in imminent danger of being crushed in their conflict. The cold was excessive. Frankenstein had daily declined in health: a feverish fire still glimmered in his eyes; but his life force was exhausted, and when suddenly roused to any exertion, he speedily returned into torpor.

One morning as I watched his wan countenance — his eyes half closed, his limbs hanging listlessly — I was roused by half a dozen of the sailors, who demanded admission into the cabin. They entered, and their leader addressed me. He and his companions had been chosen by the other sailors to come in deputation to me, to make me a requisition, which, in justice, I could not refuse. We were immured in ice, and should probably never escape; but they feared that if, as was possible, the ice should dissipate and a free passage be opened, I should be rash enough to continue my voyage, and lead them into fresh dangers. They insisted, therefore, that I should engage with a solemn promise, that if the vessel should be freed I would instantly direct my course southwards.

This speech troubled me. I had not despaired; nor had I yet conceived the idea of returning, if set free. Yet could I, in justice, or even in possibility, refuse this demand? I hesitated before I answered; when Frankenstein, who had at first been silent, and, indeed, appeared hardly to have force enough to attend, now roused himself; his eyes sparkled, and his cheeks flushed with momentary vigour. Turning towards the men, he said —

"What do you mean? What do you demand of your captain? Are you then so easily turned from your design? Did you not call this a glorious expedition? And wherefore was it glorious? Not because the way was smooth and placid as a southern sea, but because it was full of dangers and terror; because at every new incident your fortitude was to be called forth, and your courage exhibited; because danger and death surrounded it, and these you were to brave and over-come. For this was it a glorious, for this was it an honourable undertaking. You were hereafter to be hailed as the benefactors of your species; your names adored, as belonging to brave men who encountered death for honour, and the benefit of mankind. And now, behold, with the first imagination of danger, or, if you will, the first mighty and terrific trial of your courage, you shrink away, and are con-tent to be handed down as men who had not strength enough to endure cold and peril; and so, poor souls, they were chilly and returned to their warm firesides. Why, that requires not this preparation; ye need not have come thus far, and dragged your captain to the shame of a defeat, merely to prove yourself cowards. Oh! be men, or be more than men. Be steady to your purposes, and firm as a rock. This ice is not made of such stuff as your hearts may be; it is mutable, and cannot withstand you, if you say that it shall not. Do not return to your families with the stigma of disgrace marked on your brows. Return as heroes who have fought and conquered, and who know not what it is to turn their backs on the foe."

He spoke this with a voice so modulated to the different feelings expressed in his speech, with an eye so full of lofty design and heroism, that can you wonder that these men were moved? They looked at one another, and were unable to reply. I spoke; I told them to retire, and consider of what had been said: that I would not lead them further north if they strenuously desired the contrary; but that I hoped that, with reflection, their courage would return.

They retired, and I turned towards my friend, but he was sunk in languor, and almost deprived of life.

It is far easier, Margaret, to refuse the man of honour when he lies mute and unseen than when he holds your eye direct. What the men could not stomach in the bright glare of Frankenstein's gaze, they could more easily swallow in his absence. In a sunset encounter on the quarterdeck, they insisted they would not be swayed; and with my gallant champion all but interred below, I consented to the return. Thus were my hopes dashed by cowardice and indecision.

September 9th, the ice began to move, and roarings like thunder were heard at a distance, as the islands split and cracked in every direction. We were in the most imminent peril; but, as we could only remain passive, my chief attention was occupied by my most unfortunate guest, who the prior days had been entirely confined to his bed, drifting in and out of the waking world. The ice cracked behind us, and was driven with force towards the north; a breeze sprung from the west, and on the 11th the passage towards the south became perfectly free. When the sailors saw this, and that their return to their native country was apparently assured, a shout of tumultuous joy broke from them, loud and long-continued. Frankenstein, who was dozing, awoke and asked the cause of the tumult. "They shout," I said, "because they will soon return to their homes."

"Do you then really return?"

"Alas! yes; I cannot withstand their demands. I cannot lead them unwillingly to danger, and I must return."

"Do so if you will; but I will not. You may give up your purpose, but mine is assigned to me by Heaven, and I dare not. I must make amends with this creature. I am weak; but surely the spirits who assist me will endow me with sufficient strength. I have done him grievous harm. Through no fault of his own he is horribly marred; and I have left him without guidance or succor and have abandoned him to the ignorant mobs, at whose hands he has been harried and beaten, falsely accused of heinous crimes, and banished to the cold and the wilds. He flees me still, despairing of any measure of kindness, from me or from any of our kind. He may yet be noble of character; I must make the intercept before he acts rashly enough to cut his own life short for the fault of others." Saying this, he endeavoured to spring from the bed, but the exertion was too great for him; he fell back and fainted.

It was long before he was restored; and I often thought that life was entirely extinct. At length he opened his eyes; he breathed with difficulty, and was unable to speak. The surgeon gave him a composing draught, and ordered us to leave him undisturbed. In the mean time he told me that my friend had certainly not many hours to live.

His sentence was pronounced; and I could only grieve, and be patient. I sat by his bed, watching him; his eyes were closed, and I thought he slept; but presently he called to me in a feeble voice, and bidding me come near, said —

"Alas! the strength I relied upon is gone; I feel that I shall soon die, and he to survive me. During these last days I have been occupied in examining my past conduct; and I judge it thoroughly contemptible. In a fit of prolonged madness I created a rational creature; thereupon I was bound towards him, to assure, as far as was in my power, his happiness and well-being. This was my duty, and in the face of it I fled, as would the lowest of cowards, and hoped to face it no more. Just when the creature was most vulnerable and most impressionable, I shirked my obligation, betraying him and my own honour in the bargain. I was fully justified in not creating a companion for this first creature, even in the face of my solemn promise to do so; but it was entirely my doing that his loneliness and exile made the cause so paramount to his wretched heart.

"Long now have I chased the creature, driven in equal parts by the yearning for my own atonement and for the salvation and reconciliation of that wretched soul. That yearning has been to me as my lash to the dogs. He views me, quite justly, as his betrayer and tormentor, and eludes me at all costs, thinking I bring him only more of what has come before, or death itself. Alas! to think that he shall carry on to the end ignorant of my true purpose. Think not, Walton, that in the last moments of my existence I harbor any trace of the contempt and disgust I once did for this creature. I feel only compassion, and perhaps some measure of a father's love. The task of his enlightenment was mine, and I have failed as wretchedly as failure will allow."

I copied these passages in great wonderment. Just as Frankenstein, by his labours, could drag me from oblivion into the grey bloom of an ill-fated future, so could Walton, with the mere strokes of a quill, strip away the darkest chapters of my past. Thus were my crimes left unspoken, even undone! And thus did my creator pursue me, not with a hateful and murderous intent, but with a heart bent to compassion and salvation, and a mind set on atonement and reconciliation! Nothing could less accurately have described my history, or his true purpose, but the milky fluid poured from my eyes nonetheless; it was all I could do to prevent its smudging the page. I, who had been received so monstrously in every quarter, was quite possibly sympathetic, even noble in character. The poignancy was all but impossible to resist. Walton observed me with a tender countenance; but his thoughts were on Frankenstein. "It's a tale of repentance and valiantly attempted restitution," he said. "And all the more heroic for its failure."

"I would implore you, Captain Walton, to undertake my unfinished work... Yet I cannot ask you to renounce your country and friends to fulfill this task; and now that you are returning to England you will have little chance of meeting with him. But the consideration of these points, and the well balancing of what you may esteem your duties, I leave to you; my judgment and ideas are already disturbed by the near approach of death."

His voice became faint as he spoke; and at length, exhausted by his effort, he sunk into silence. About half an hour afterwards he attempted again to speak, but was unable; he pressed my hand feebly, and his eyes closed forever, while the irradiation of a gentle smile passed away from his lips.

That very night, as if Frankenstein had willed it from the place beyond, I encountered this very creature. I entered the cabin where lay the remains of my ill-fated and admirable friend. Over him hung a form which I cannot find words to describe: — gigantic in stature, and uncouth, his face concealed by long locks of ragged hair. One vast hand was extended, in colour and apparent texture like that of a mummy. When he heard the sounds of my approach, he ceased to utter exclamations of grief and horror, and sprung towards the window. Never did I behold a vision so horrible as his face, its ill-favored features distorted all the more for its obvious long-suffering. I shut my eyes, involuntarily, and endeavoured to recollect what were my duties with regard to this wretched creature. I called on him to stay.

I had no plan of action, but only the vaguest sense of purpose. Unbeknownst to my crew, who would most certainly have killed the creature on sight, I harboured him in my cabin as quietly as I could manage, struggling to collect my racing thoughts while fearing not immoderately for my own wellbeing, if not my life. And yet common ground stretched between us; we were both reeling in exhaustion, in fear, and in grief — for in the end he loved his creator as I did. Once his own fears were calmed he made no obnoxious demonstration of his physical superiority. On the contrary, he spoke in the most civilized manner, and even yielded me the first turn on the bed. As we took our respective bouts of long slumber, the seeds were sown for something approaching a mutual understanding. Somewhere between sleep and waking, my own vision for a course of action became clear. I saw the creature as some part gentleman and some part brute; he differed not so much in that regard from most men. But by any reckoning, he comprised a scientific marvel; my solemn duty lay in his safe delivery to the enlightened arms of learned men. The violence of my ignorant crew posed his most immediate threat; my initial instinct to conceal him had been correct, and maintaining his concealment through the balance of the journey was my foremost concern.

From the creature's view, awaking in the relative comfort of my cabin, fed and looked after as the guest of a man who'd not betrayed him to an easily assembled mob, was a revelation in itself. Despite what everything in his wretched past had taught him of the cruelty and treachery of man, he accepted my plan without reservation.

And so we settled into our journey southward, a journey destined otherwise to have been insufferable, my expedition aborted without the slightest scientific contribution, and I the laughing stock of all explorers. Instead, unbeknownst to my most unworthy crew, I shared my cabin with the most significant scientific finding since the debunking of flat Earth.

Through the outlay of some not insubstantial sterling, I prevailed upon the crew, mutinous curs that they be, to deliver us to London, and then to return the ship to Archangel under the guidance of my second-in-command. Such was the creature's natural proclivity to the workings of the sailing ship, that he and I handled that vessel of considerable scale, in exclusion of all other seamen, every night watch for the duration of our journey. I should also mention that though the creature had led a bitter rough life, and all the more so of late, he wasted not a moment of his newfound leisure in idleness, but applied every free waking hour most diligently, to his learning in mathematics and the letters, both of which I oversaw with great satisfaction. Indeed, Margaret, he is nearly my equal in trigonometry; and so far has his writing progressed, I would soon have him compose you a letter!

Upon our arrival at the London docks, he and I alighted under cover of darkness. We made our way through the city on foot, with but one unfortunate incident, the nature of which I shall not relate here. We settled thereupon, and remain still, in my house. Stripped as it is of all staff, we are forced to make our own subsistence; at this we have so far succeeded.

I have taken to calling him Franz. He continues his education while I prepare his and his creator's astonishing story for publication. He has become a great help to me even in that endeavour, functioning quite ably as copy clerk. As I'm sure you've surmised from its unfamiliar script, this very letter is copied by his hand.

The clock strikes 7:00; I must adjourn for the evening meal. It is prepared by the creature himself, and quite competently, if recent history serves as a guide.

Again, Margaret, you must pledge your confidentiality on all of these matters until you have my advice to the contrary. For obvious reasons I am currently unable to travel, but I anticipate with great pleasure our rendezvous at the earliest opportunity.

Your affectionate brother,

Robert Walton

Chapter IX

Cloaked as it was, and with oil lamps burning round-the-clock, the house had a stale and timeless air. Only the hourly chimes suggested the passage of days and prompted us to our steady labours. The manuscript now occupied all of Walton's attention. Not until his second ream of paper had he understood the magnitude of his task. "Much as I revered the man, Frankenstein's viewpoint was distorted by the time he reached our boat. The physical and mental strain of the chase was altogether too much. And from the narrative standpoint, there's the great inconvenience that he knew so little about you, just as you were so largely ignorant about him."

That was more true than I would once have believed. The weeks with Walton had taught me something about actually knowing a man; and, by contrast, how little I'd really known of my creator. In years of tortured contemplation, I'd conjured his whole being from just a few paltry hours of conversation, and from actions I'd not fully comprehended. I'd watched him, for days and weeks on end; but to watch a man at distance, or through the silent glass, is not to know him. While far from a blank page, he was a man of more possibility than I'd imagined.

Walton's narrative shift required him to collate all the many aspects of the tale. Accordingly, he began to press me on the matter of my personal history, with the quite understandable air that mine was just one of several possible points of view, each of them perfectly viable. The accounts of my early life largely matched Frankenstein's, and seemed to satisfy Walton as well. But he questioned me relentlessly on those parts of the story he liked least, as if in the constant retelling something essential might be altered. I related events as memory allowed, while leaving, as best I could, some margin for interpretation.

For as long as I'd awaited and pondered it, my wardrobe arrived with shocking abruptness, a sudden rap at the door that jolted us both upright. Walton slipped outside to speak with the driver, reappeared with an armload of boxes, and made two repeat trips with similar bounty. With every pass, the door admitted unaccustomed shafts of sunlight. The driver held to his carriage, and I to the interior shadows, barely able to contain my anticipation. "One more," Walton indicated, but as he turned to the door, the driver poked in, startling the both of us for a second time, dropping the last box, and taking a quick look about.

"Is that your Uncle Franz?" he asked, after what I took to be an awkward silence.

"It is. You've quite a memory," said Walton, dispatching him with a coin and shutting the door quickly behind him. "What are the chances?" he muttered with a grimace and a short string of curses as the carriage wheels rattled off. For my part, I was as stunned with the repeated admissions and withdrawals of sunlight, as with the half-glimpse the driver had caught of me. And my eagerness for the clothing quickly outpaced them both. "Well, I suppose there's nothing to be done now," Walton conceded. "Let's see to the packages."

Each box was tied in decorative twine, and each item within draped in exotic paper with a luxurious feel and a lovely scent. Walton supervised the unwrapping, and took pains to explain the workings and care of each garment; but when it came time for the fitting, I preferred the privacy of my own chamber. I emerged some time later, to great fanfare from Walton, whose mood had largely recovered. He held a glass of wine, unusual for that time of day, and goaded me to extended parading.

Elegant clothing transformed my outlook well beyond my most immodest expectations. The comfort of the undergarments was a constant source of amazement, both in the softness of the fabric and the support it provided where I'd had none before. Gone were the pinching, chafing, and clamping that had long plagued my movement, and with them some measure of my awkwardness and surly demeanour. Walton pointed out that such undergarments were not commonly worn, and that most men, Walton among them, relied on long shirt-tails to "protect one's backside from the scratch of wool trousers, and the wool, in turn, from the unseemliness of one's backside." As to my primary garments, Walton observed that, even days later, I lingered at the mirror "like a rose-cheeked bridesmaid"; and when I left it, not a minute went by without my eye fastening on some aspect of my finely clad periphery. Bare limbs protruding from the house-gown had bothered me but slightly; beyond the furs I'd fashioned in the north, I'd never had sleeves or pants of anywhere near proper length. But now I loathed that gangly aspect in its absence; exquisitely tailored sleeves, and pant legs descending to well-shined boots, fairly shouted of my reinvention. I felt it in my every occupation, and took new care to conduct myself in the more dignified manner now indicated; to avoid, where possible, ungainly movements; to avoid soiling myself in the kitchen or about any of my other chores; and to further emphasize my other more sophisticated endeavours. My contributions as clerk had long surpassed simple copying, but now I supplemented corrections of grammar and sequence with the more subtle excursions into meter, voice, and tone. And, at Walton's prompting, I embarked on my much-contemplated correspondence with Mrs. Saville. "Margaret has but few acquaintances," he said by way of final authorization, "and in her station, she depends on my full devotion. I've been unable to supply it in person, and have done so but sporadically in writing. She could use the distraction, you the experience, and I the balm to my conscience."

But nowhere was my transformation so evident as in my role as Walton's companion at table, where the conversation turned from alternately dissertational and inquisitional to something near congenial. At the approach of the evening meal, Walton generally concerned himself with the wine, enquiring as to what food I'd be serving and choosing the bottle that best matched it from his cellar reserves. He'd uncork and decant, consume a glass before the meal and several more while eating. During the early days of my stay he accepted my reluctance to drink along with him; but this changed dramatically when I discarded the ludicrous house-gown. Arrayed as I was in fresh linens and a fine dark suit, Walton's entreaties, quite naturally, acquired a more pressing tone. He claimed it dishonorable to leave one's host to drink alone, and carried on so that, in the face of such an onslaught, I complied as best I could within certain levels of prudence, steadily developing both my taste and my tolerance.

"At your size you should be drinking twice what I do," he said, "but you're lucky if you're drinking half." Still, he seemed pleased with my modest concessions to fellowship; I'd not liked wine when I'd tasted it as a younger creature, and I'll admit to some enjoyment in the reintroduction, not only for its sweet flavour, but for the sense of long-borne heaviness lifting off me in bits and pieces. I paid less mind to Walton's speech in those moments and indulged more in my own musings. I recall in particular admiring the passage of the table candles, the flow of wax through the channels in their rims, down their sides, and into the metal intricacies of the candelabra. I fancied that I began to understand certain qualities of Walton's humour. And I began to link certain elements of my experience with corresponding elements of my education; to recognize episodes of cause and effect I hadn't quite grasped before. Some of these revelations seemed so significant it was all I could do not to interrupt the meal to take up paper and quill. I resisted that as a requirement of decorum, but every attempt to recreate my thoughts at a later time fell strangely short, indicating either an odd failing at their recollection, or an exaggerated initial conception of their worth; I was never quite sure which.

To Walton's credit, he never drank before the 6:00 bell, and never approached the state I'd observed in the men who'd accosted us in the laneway. But at the end of the evenings a certain disorder could be detected in his movements, and a corresponding sluggishness to his tongue. My reaction was not one of disgust or distaste, but rather of assistance and forbearance, as one presented with the opportunity to repay some small measure of one's debt. And yet, the moment I'd seen him safely to bed I had a keen awareness, something nearing urgency, that my time at last was my own; and I felt myself beset with strangely powerful yearnings not present during the routines of the day. Some were new pleasures easily satisfied: bathing, for example, and the joy of taking a book into bed, legs beneath the bedclothes, down pillows propped at my back, three burning candles and a glass of wine on the side table, a leather volume propped in my lap. Some were remembered pleasures currently unattainable: the light of the sun and the feel of its warmth upon my flesh, the cool forest breeze to temper it, the nightly pageant of the moon and the stars, the scent of the earth and the tread of it beneath my feet. And some were sensations more remote and disturbing, welling deep within me, and for which I had no words.

Chapter X

November 17th, 17——

Dear Mrs Saville:

By now, I trust, you will have received Captain Walton's letter of introduction. I beg your forbearance with one so artless in the ways of society, and so particularly inexperienced in the way of correspondence.

I cannot overstate the kindness of your brother in seeing to my safety, my sustenance, and my education, taking me first into his captain's quarters, and then into his home. Though wholly unfamiliar with the ways of domestic life, I have endeavoured to assimilate the skills required to run the household in something of the manner to which he is accustomed. I flatter myself to consider this, and my work as his copy clerk, to be of some use to him as he labours to bring the manuscript into an acceptable form.

Your brother has always spoken of you in the highest regard, and while I wouldn't presume to speak for such a man, I dare say he counts the days until he sees you once again in person.

Your humble servant,

Franz P. Frankenstein

I'd not much taken to "Franz." And Frankenstein, in a strictly bio-
logical sense, had no claim to my surname. But as Walton pointed
out, what person has any say in his given name? And what father
had ever played a more comprehensive role in the formation of succeeding life than Frankenstein in mine? As to the letter P, it signi-
fied nothing beyond Walton's insistence that a man of any breeding
must carry at least one initial, and preferably more. In his lighter
moments, he would banter with certain derivatives – Phineas,
Peerless, Paxton – but in the end would allow only that P provided
the most assertive plosive between the two fricatives, *Franz* and
Frankenstein. Knowing nothing of such matters, I had no basis for
disagreement.

November 21st, 17—

My Dear Franz:

*It was a delight to hear from one of whom my brother has written so glow-
ingly, who has improved himself against such overwhelming odds, and whose
origin is both poignant and fascinating beyond all description. As someone
my brother has esteemed sufficiently to take into his sea cabin and his London
home, you are most deserving of my own personal esteem and all that entails. I understand that this sentiment may stand in contrast to your prior
experiences with mankind, and so much the better for that. Would I be overly
presumptuous to apologize, on behalf of all humanity, for the cruel subjection
of your early years? And to wish you, with all of my heart, the happiest of
lives going forward?*

*As to the manner in which my brother is accustomed to having his house-
hold managed, you should rest easy in the knowledge that his former staff were
sluggards and slobs to a one; and the lifeless clay that passed for cooking in his
house was nothing short of repulsive.*

As an aside, I must gently admonish you never to address me as Mrs Saville.

I detest the moniker nearly as much as the man from whom it derives. I am Margaret to you here forward.

Yours fondly,

Margaret

My Dear Margaret (if I may):

It is a great honour to have a letter from you, and an unprecedented delight to have such kind words. I value them beyond my ability to describe.

As a response to your gentle aside, my own moniker is not much to my liking, but nowhere near to the point of detestation. I'm sorry to hear of your own distress on the matter, and, of course, will readily comply with your wishes.

I am also sorry, though not nearly so much, to read that your brother's poor eating predated his latest voyage. Even I, one who has scavenged the most barren landscapes for what bitter scraps might be foraged, found the maritime fare to be much lacking. The contribution of such a diet to the poor performance of the men was the topic of some spirited discussion between us. As to our current table, we have reached something of a middle ground. My own disinclination to animal flesh, or meat, as Captain Walton prefers to call it, has nudged him into my own realm of plants and nuts. And his own disinclination to raw fare has nudged me into the realm of cooking those items, though not in the hideous manner to which he was previously accustomed, drowned overlong in boiling water. Oiled, seasoned, and directly exposed to the dry heat of flame has proven the more palatable approach, and we are each of us accordingly satisfied. He reports an improved overall aspect, particularly in the matter of regular and satisfying defecation; and if an improved diet has played some small part in that, then I am doubly pleased. Please rest assured that his spirits remain as robust as his physical health while he continues to develop the manuscript.

Yours fondly,

Franz

November 29th, 17——

My Dear Franz:

I was particularly edified by your accounts of Captain Walton's performance in the areas of digestion and defecation. God speed to you both on such matters.

As to the preparation of vegetables, I too abhor them boiled to tasteless mush, but Mr Saville, of course, will have them no other way.

If he were anyone but himself, my title would be but indifferent to me. However, and as I'm sure Robert has described, I bear the name of a brute, a bully, and a boor. And stranded here in the country, rarely venturing from this accursed chair or this accursed house, I am afforded little else in the way of company; that is, unless one would so consider the teated sow or the carbunkled cow. But such are my affairs that the chance barnyard beast is a much-treasured relief to the inane blather and incessant hectoring of that man, my husband. And yet, no sooner do I betray the slightest affection for such a beast, than he puts it to the slaughter, subjecting me to its plaintive shrieks and hanging it to bleed at the center of my only prospect to the outdoors. He would have it ever known that he is the iron-fisted master of both my person and this measly domain, as befits the most highly self-esteemed Charles Edwin Saville III, or Captain Saville, as he bids me address him.

Yours very fondly,

Margaret

Chapter XI

"Your sister seems both unhappily wed and unnaturally anchored."

Walton moved the food around his plate. His eating had dropped off of late, and while it was difficult to ascertain by candlelight, a pallor in his face seemed recently to have joined the drooping beneath his eyes. "Anchored she is," he said at last, taking a long swill from his glass. "Like you here in some respects, though your confinement is but temporary." He eyed me with a certain significance. "You'll learn that women, even in the best of conditions, do not simply stroll out of their marriages; nor do they change their stations by setting off across the countryside, as you were long disposed to do. And Margaret, I'm afraid, is not a woman in the best of conditions. From birth, she's suffered with clubfoot, or clubfeet, as it were; she struggles to cross the room, let alone the country. Her plight was compounded in early childhood when my dolt of a father spilt a pot of tea and rather badly burned her face and neck. Her prospects for a decent marriage, never particularly bright on account of her feet, were much worsened by that calamity. And so it was that she ended with a man as vile as Saville."

"I knew nothing of this."

"Would that she'd not married at all. He's brutish in both temperament and physique, retired from what I understand to be particularly undistinguished service in the army, where the only skill he seems to have acquired is an ongoing appetite for savagery. He has her on a piece of land carved from a bog; "Sweetbriar," he calls it. He fancies it an estate, though nothing of any value grows there, but rather, festers. The house is of dank and mouldering stone, unnaturally lacking in sunlight, and cold the year round. He allows no domestic staff, though to do so would be well within his means, and confines her to performing its many labours. When he does go off on some nefarious business or other, he leaves her under the watch of two monstrous dogs in whose presence she quite rightly fears for her life. And yet she much prefers that condition to the norm, with her husband at hand to actively torment her."

"Can't something be done?"

"Meddling in someone else's marriage is a dangerous business, Franz, not that I haven't tried. He's a short-tempered brute, and experience shows it would end by his killing me, and probably her in the bargain; or by my killing him, with my own life then forfeit by way of the hangman's noose." He finished his glass, ahead of his normal pace, and poured another for each of us. "I would almost do it, so much do I loathe the man and esteem my dear sister, but what life would await her then? A badly scarred half-cripple, disgraced and marooned, no one left to her in this world. Would that I could slay just one to your five, and walk as free as you have."

Something unintended sounded in my throat, and I turned away as we drained our glasses.

"My apologies, Franz," he said after a moment. "Wine has made loose with my tongue. Scandalous neglect and hideous mistreatment drove you to those murders; or you were provoked and knew no better. Quite understandable in either case."

The killings, I'll confess, were not much in my mind; nor had they ever been, beyond the effect of the first three on my creator, which I'd absolutely intended, and the threat of them all to Walton's schemes for our future. On moral grounds I cared not a whit, and thus did Walton's absolution mean little to me. Only later did it occur to me that in our earliest encounters I could very easily have killed Walton himself, and, in my ignorance of his person, would have done so with an equal lack of regret. For now though, my thoughts were engaged in curious resentment at that same Walton, the first I'd harboured against him since I'd cuffed him at the boat rail; not at his loose mention of my crimes, but at his notion that I'd ever had the pleasure to "walk free." Yes, I'd roamed the wilderness as Margaret could never. But one who spends his life in hiding, as I'd done in all my time there, and did still in that very house, cannot be said to walk free.

"The good news," he continued, "is that by the great fortune of Frankenstein's private nature, he would not divulge anything of his work until the living proof of it was far from reach. The ravings of a madman to a disbelieving Irish magistrate, and to an equally disbelieving Genevan magistrate – they're as nothing; we're the only two with any real grasp of your crimes. And by virtue of our literary labours, we expunge those within these walls, for all eternity. A drink to that!"

Walton was in bed well before the appointed hour of 11:00. I felt, more keenly than ever, my great debt for his reclaiming me from the depths of despair, and my satisfaction, beyond any prior hope, in my occupation, in the fellowship of his company, and in this infinitely higher mode of life; and yet I knew what I was about as if I'd planned it for weeks. Ignoring the tubful of pots and crockery, I threw a cloak about my shoulders, unlatched the back door and ducked through. The alley, I knew, presented far less exposure than the street. Only a small band of sky was available to me in that narrow vista, but even there the stars shone as I'd left them so long before, brilliant and beyond count. I breathed the cool air and felt the life in my legs, working briskly down the alley to the east. My eyes adjusted to the moonless night as they'd done over so many nights in the wild. Experience had shown that my night vision surpassed that of most men, though whether this was a matter of makeup or of long custom was unclear to me. Dogs were my only accosters; for the most part they dispersed when I feinted at them.

Since my initial flight from Ingolstadt as a hulking eight-footer with the clueless and all-fearing mind of a motherless babe, I'd barely strolled the most meager of man's encampments. By the hard-learned mandate of self-preservation, I'd ventured into the chance village only as required by desperate hunger or by the various labours of Frankenstein's torment. Now, of my own volition, I walked the largest, densest city I'd ever imagined, where the homes piled together in long continuous runs, featureless masses holding people in unthinkable numbers, capable at any breach of massing against me. I felt surprisingly little fear at the notion; once you've reckoned on the pitiless pyre, the common mob holds less terror than it did before. But I held to that alleyway and skipped quickly by the cross streets, partly out of respect for Walton – bad enough that I'd left the house without my now taking additional risks of discovery; and partly for fear of losing myself once I'd veered off the straight path, so strangely bereft was the scene of trees, rock formations, and gradations in the landscape that might guide my return. The air, so bracing on my first exposure, revealed itself on certain blocks as a miasma of coal smoke, urine, and rot. And still, there was great pleasure in my first venture outdoors after so long, and my first ever in boots and proper clothing, both of which were holding up nicely on their first real test.

After a league or so, I began my return. I'd seen a few people in windows, and a few huddling near their doors, but none, to my knowledge had noticed me in the dark. The same blocks brought the same barking dogs; they were just as easily deterred on the second encounter. Dogs had been a torment to me all my life, less for attacking than for alerting the locals. My experience with the sledge dogs in the far north had changed all that; they were the first creatures on this earth to make any sustained effort on my behalf, and their selfless exertions, over so many leagues in such hostile conditions, were enough to touch my long-blackened soul. Even if I'd been inclined to eat dog, which I wasn't and had never been, I'd have released them when I did, to give them what chance they retained for survival. But when a dog leapt out now, a large one, flat-eared and short-haired, having lain in wait like the daemon he was, and quickly tore a chunk of my new trousers over the boot, I had no qualms at swift retribution. I kicked a good crack in its ribs, and considered, with some satisfaction, that the boots had just served doubly, saving me a wound and enhancing the impact of my riposte. The dog, though suffering, showed no ebb in its resolve, backing low, barking madly and readying to spring again. Instead, and to its surprise, it was I who sprung, collaring it in an armlock, its teeth snapping near my face, and working one hand onto each jaw so that one set of teeth impressed the underside of each set of fingers. With my leverage secured, I wrenched the bottom from the top in one violent motion, the sound of it so near my ear cracking like musket fire.

Quiet resumed its hold on the night. The barking had ceased; the creature lay in a rapid silent pant, its jaw hideously and forever agape. I picked it up by the paws, tossed it whence it had come, and resumed my pace to Walton's door.

December 3rd, 17——

My Dear Margaret:

I am greatly distressed to read of your plight. Your description of the cruel and ill-meaning slaughter reveals a coldness in your husband's heart I cannot begin to fathom. And your stranding in such miserable circumstance is enough to break my own.

In some ways, I too have been stranded, and for the whole of my life. For years I trudged in the prison of my own enforced solitude; and when finally favoured with the company of your admirable brother, I'm squirreled away in a tiny ship's cabin or in this ever-darkened house, barred from the pageant of life in the eternal avoidance of discovery. Captain Walton, whom I trust implicitly in these matters, judges it still unsafe to venture out, even under cover of darkness, until the time is right and the proper arrangements have been secured. I will, however, confess, if only to you, of my stepping into the unpopulated alley the night before last for a breath of fresh air and a glimpse at the stars. The latter, I am happy to report, were still arrayed in all their glory.

I write of my own seclusion only to imply some small understanding of your own; it is far from my intent to equate our stations. Surely your misery exceeds mine by a great margin; one must simply compare the company of Captain Walton, whom I esteem above all men, to that of Mr Saville, whose loathsome presence you quite rightly revile.

Would that I could be of even the slightest service to you. I would hold it far above any service to myself.

Yours very fondly,

Franz

Chapter XII

"Forgive me," I said, having first chewed and swallowed in accordance with the rules of civility, "but last night's discussion of Margaret and her husband has left me wondering as to the exact nature of marriage."

"Hah!" said Walton, "There's a question!" He considered me as if for the first time. "And not one to be undertaken on empty glasses." He pushed back his dinner plate and poured out the rest of the bottle.

"Having never undergone the sacrifice of matrimony, I answer not from personal experience, but merely as an observer of the human condition, and as an inexpert devotee of the natural sciences. Putting aside the horror of Margaret and Saville, and describing the condition more generally, marriage is a convention developed over the millenia to impose some order on the reproductive process. It's a central tenet in humanity's claim to moral superiority over the rest of the animal kingdom. Without it, or so the argument goes, we'd be reduced to savagery, men slaying one another over access to certain women, women used and abandoned, children left wanting and uncared for. Instead, by its virtues, we have couples committing for life, one man to one woman, and one woman to one man, the ceremony overseen in tandem by both of our dominant institutions, the church and the state."

"How then does this arrangement enable reproduction?"

"The natural process is then free to take its course. Marriage has delayed it only until such time as certain requirements have been met

— rightful ages attained, permissions granted, financial minimums attained and demonstrated."

"To what natural process do you refer?"

"Why, copulation Franz!" We pondered each other for a long moment. "Have you not, in all your travels, acquired any familiarity with its doings? Never observed the coupling of two sparrows? Never watched a buck mount a doe, a stallion a mare, a ram a ewe?"

Suddenly it was perfectly clear, my whole worldview altered in a matter of seconds. "I happened once upon two dogs... I admit I'd never quite pieced it together."

Walton clapped me on the shoulder. "You mean in all your haranguing of Frankenstein to create you a mate, you hadn't such activity in mind?"

"Not for a moment. Only simple company and comfort. It seemed the natural course."

"Nothing could be more unnatural!"

"You yourself are not married, despite having attained what I assume to be a rightful age and suitable fortune. So it follows that you have no more experience with copulation than I?"

"But there you may be overlooking certain attributes particular to my person."

"I'm afraid I don't follow."

"I'm generally considered to be rather strikingly handsome."

Never having considered that, I studied him for a moment.

"Forgive me, but I don't see that."

"It's perfectly natural that you lack refinement in areas of aesthetic judgment."

"Am I then to infer that you have engaged in copulation, despite the marital prerequisite?"

"This is hardly the conversation of polite table, Franz. Honour permits me to say only this: life brings exception to most every rule."

"How does honour enter in? Surely nothing could be less dignified than what I saw of those dogs."

"And therein, I suppose, lies your answer."

December 7th, 17—

My Dear Franz:

Your kind letters are an immeasurable service to me in their own right. I long for them in their passage, and treasure them on their arrival. Your fidelity as a correspondent is already most happily known to me, and as such I fear not that you will fail to write. I fear only that my vile husband will intercept the precious pages and most cruelly withhold them. He is barely literate, and to date has shown little interest in my correspondence generally, or in that from you specifically, that is, beyond the question of the unfamiliar hand, which I've quite truthfully attributed to the able clerk my brother has engaged to chronicle his seafaring adventures. But in this, as in all things, he requires no motive beyond spite, and is most eager to deprive me of what I desire most; accordingly I feign but little interest in your pages, while poring endlessly over them in my private moments. Owing to my condition, the regular postman, the dear Mr Garvey, is kind enough to deliver direct to my hand; but he is entitled to occasional leave, and is sometimes assigned to other temporary duties. Those are the days I fear most.

The "ever darkened house" you mention is surely an affliction we suffer in common. I've ever abhorred those horrid curtains my brother so admires; and never, on my visits, would I tolerate them drawn while the sun still shone, however faint its effects in that coal-clouded city. Sweetbriar, as my husband so ludicrously calls it, could be the sunniest place in all England for what little I see of it. The house is well enough appointed with windows, but they're smothered with such a hideous tangle of overgrowth that I hardly know night from day. Its thorns are sufficient to form many thousands of Christ's crowns, and so am I tormented in looking endlessly upon it. But I've long since desisted in the request that my husband make the removal; the more he gleans the nature of my desire, the less likely he is to undertake it.

As to my own condition, I'm sure my brother has mentioned the deformity of my feet and the hellish scarring of my face. While both have contributed to my poor station, only the former remains a plague to me. I avoid the looking glass as a matter of course, and, beyond the kind Mr Garvey, I encounter none but my loathsome husband, in whose case I am actually pleased to present the hideous countenance he so richly deserves.

Yours very fondly,

Margaret

December 10th, 17—

My Dear Margaret:

Such a beast as Saville deserves no such thing as to look upon your countenance. If you will forgive the impertinence, I would consider it my greatest joy to look upon you, even for a moment, not to mention basking in the exquisite company he so misguidedly abuses.

Your brother, in his letters, failed to convey the principle disagreement between my creator and me. Having seen enough of the cruelty of this world, and of my apparently solitary lot in its proceedings, I demanded that he build me a mate, a companion in this otherwise wretched life. This seemed only fair, on its own merits and by way of compensation, and he granted his solemn promise to make it so, to create my likeness in the female form. This duty he then most callously disregarded, traipsing over Europe in pursuit of his own happiness, undertaking some semblance of the project only after the passage of several months, and recklessly abandoning it shortly thereafter, in favour of resuming his own pleasures.

It was thus that I lured him northward into the most inhospitable climes,

69

for the punishment that he, in your words, so richly deserved. I undertook that journey in a state of complete despair; and yet, for all its hardships, it led me to your brother, and from your brother to you. No matter what may occur here forward, this is my enduring solace.

Sleep well, my dear Margaret, and preserve yourself until such time as our fates have appointed.

Yours very fondly,

Franz

Chapter XIII

After several months of concentrated labour, and a corresponding decline in his health and vitality, Walton declared the manuscript ready for publication. I made four copies of the initial offering letter, and addressed them to his four designees, the most prominent scientific publishers in London.

February 17th, 17—

Dear Sirs:

I am a London-based explorer, just returned from a sea journey to the far north, where I was witness to the greatest breakthrough in the modern history of science. There in the most unlikely and barren of environs I encountered the most unlikely, nay impossible, of specimens; a living, walking creature with all the apparent attributes of man, including those of reason and speech; but born of no mother, assembled rather in a laboratory of science, and animated thereupon from lifeless matter.

In the creature's pursuit was the visionary genius who, by his own hand, had brought the creature into being, who alone among all the men of scientific history, had uncovered the very elixir of life. Exhausted by prolonged exposure to the unbearable cold prevalent in those latitudes, he boarded my ship for a convalescence that would ultimately prove futile. There he related to me the tale known to no other, which I meticulously recorded in voluminous notes that he himself reviewed and supplemented where he thought necessary. He expired shortly thereupon and was buried at sea.

I have now incorporated these notes into a larger, more complete manuscript, which it is my great honour to offer you as a once in a millennium publishing opportunity. Please note that I am in possession of not just the manuscript, but of the creature himself, who returned in my ship — unknown to my crew, as I deemed them a threat to him on account of the disconcerting nature of his appearance; he resides with me even now in the most civilized manner. It is my intention to present the manuscript in person, and upon the sufficient expression of your interest, to present the creature in a private audience at a date following shortly thereafter. Please contact me at your earliest convenience with dates and times of your convenience.

Sincerely,

Robert Walton

With these posted, a great weight seemed removed from Walton's shoulders. He resumed his interest in my intellectual improvement, engaging me once again in my reading and in mathematics, though he'd little left to contribute to the latter. Perhaps by way of compensation, he introduced board and card games, chess and piquet respectively, and set the late afternoons aside for our increasingly animated contests. He paid mind to my every endeavour, much as he'd done before, even as related to the most mundane household chores. He took particular delight in activities for which I was most naturally, or unnaturally, suited. Dusting high shelves, replacing high candles, funneling fuel into high-placed oil lamps; these he observed were far more efficiently accomplished without the need for a stool. He noticed the tear in my trousers, as he hadn't before, and sent them out for repair; to preserve him from distress, I attributed it to a snag in the kitchen.

I pressed him further on Margaret, inquiring as to whether the time when we awaited the publishers' responses might not present an opportunity for his long-delayed visit. This line of questioning he more or less evaded, either from some aversion to the trip itself, which I doubted; or from a continuing unease at leaving me alone in the house for the period required, a concern he would not address, nor even admit.

"Couldn't Margaret come here then?" I asked at last. "I've no experience in such things, but I imagine a carriage could be hired and sent to her. I could remain from view as you deemed appropriate."

"She'll meet you soon enough, and won't shy from you any more than I have. But Saville would no sooner let her drive off on her own than he would join the clergy. In this case, I'll admit his position is not unique; there's not a man in all England who'd abide his wife's two-day journey, unescorted, on remote highways teeming with ruffians, thieves, and worse. But the convention suits him all too sweetly; I swear the only reason he married a clubfoot was to more effectively confine her to his domestic prison."

February 19th, 17—

My Dear Margaret:

At long last, Captain Walton's labours have reached fruition. His proposals have been dispatched to the finest publishers; he expects responses by return post and anticipates reviewing the manuscript with each of them within the fortnight. Long have I deplored the dismal effect of such unceasing application on his person, but even now the colour returns to his countenance, and good health to his features. Reputable publication promises the reward of all his long labours, not only the long months here at the parlour table, but all the long years prior, communing with nautical halfwits, supplying in dreary ports, and pitching in hostile seas.

As to my own modest prospects, publication is the necessary first step in my introduction to gentle society. As Captain Walton has said from the beginning, when my story is known, I am no longer to be reviled and beaten, but wondered at, and accepted into the better class of men. And yet, the only society for which I long is yours. Your safety and happiness are my principle concerns; and to that end, I encourage Captain Walton, with as much doggedness as I dare, to make his long overdue journey to Sweetbriar, to bring you some brief respite from your torment, and me some testament of your wellbeing. He continues to resist, I suspect for fear of leaving me here unattended. How bitter the irony, how horribly it pains me, to be the impediment to your affectionate and long overdue reunion! I endeavour daily to earn his confidence, and am not without hope that he will reconsider before long.

Yours very fondly,

Franz

Matterless Books
Drury Lane
London

February 24th, 17—

Dear Mr Walton:

We have read your proposal with great interest. Unfortunately, it is not a fit for us at this time. Of course these are largely matters of both personal taste and fiscal opportunity; other publishers may have a different response. I wish you the best of luck with your project.

Sincerely,

Aeneas P. Matterless II
Publisher

74

Scientifica Britannica
Church Street
London

February 25th, 17——

My Dear Sir:

Your proposal is best addressed elsewhere.   I might suggest Bethlem Hospital at Moorfields, which is said to have a strong trade in lunacy.

Sincerely,

Ebeneezer D. Anderson
Publisher

Sackville & Sons
Printers and Purveyors of Fine Books
Finsbury Square
London

February 27, 17–

Mr Walton:

There can be no thought of our pursuing such nonsense.

Sincerely,

Benjamin P. Sackville III
Publisher

The Worshipful Company of Stationers
Ave Maria Lane
London

February 28th, 17—

Mr Walton:

Yours is precisely the cheap, scientific fiction that impugns the reputation of those who publish works of genuine academic integrity. Your ruse is laughably transparent, with the convenient death of the man behind the miracle, the equally convenient lack of any witnesses aboard ship, and, no doubt, some poseur standing by to play the creature. Do you take us for such fools, sir? May I remind you that we have built one of the world's most esteemed publishing enterprises, while you, an ostensible pursuer of the world's great wonders, are but the laughable purveyor of its basest fiction.

Sincerely,

George C. Pomeranz
Publisher

Walton had read the first three letters aloud, with admirable composure and even some hint of good humour. But the last he read to himself, his jaw tightening as if upon a thin strip of leather. "Pomeranz envisions a poseur," he said at last, folding the letter and setting it on the table. "Perhaps it's time we made him an introduction."

Chapter XIV

Walton hired a carriage for Ave Maria Lane the very next morning and was engaged there for most of the day. It was the longest he'd left me alone in the house, and while I had a thought or two about poking into the alley during the sunlit hours, I dared not take the chance. The best I could muster was to prop open the back door to admit a bit of fresh air and a shaft of sunlight while I went about my kitchen duties.

Walton returned after dark, but well in time for his wine before dinner. From the day I'd taken over all food preparation he'd avoided the kitchen altogether, just as he'd avoided my sleeping chamber, ceding them both as areas of my exclusive domain. He stood now in the doorway, leaning on the jamb and cradling his glass.

"As I mentioned last night, it seems we need to reverse our preferred order of events, that is to say, effect your introduction to Pomeranz as a means to his interest in the manuscript, rather than as a reward for it. As such, I've hired a carriage for tomorrow afternoon. I'll drive it myself. You'll ride in back on a mattress, under a blanket. Consider it your beauty rest. I've now had a good look at the building, and I know exactly where Pomeranz sits. I'll work my way into his office just after dark. You'll conceal yourself outside in the rear alley; he's three flights up, but I know you're a particularly able climber. When I open the window, you'll make your entry, and take your further cues from me."

And so it was that, at about the time I would normally begin my preparations for the evening meal, Walton pulled the carriage up the alley, and, having scanned in both directions, I scampered out into it. The ride, I knew, would be long and jolty, but the mattress and blanket made it but a gentle rocking; I allowed myself the imagining of a mother rocking my infant form in her slender arms, a sight such as I'd lingered over more than once with a great pang in my heart. I awoke from an unusually pleasing slumber to Walton's peeling away the blanket. The night had set in, but my eyes quickly adjusted to the task at hand, a three-storey climb to the well-lit office Walton indicated. The alley was quiet, and I set at once to the chore as Walton made his way to the front.

The building offered a wealth of holds; a few gaps in the stone were all I required; decorative architraves and cornices were great luxuries even to one as recently unpracticed as I. The principal challenge lay in preserving my clothes; I'd chosen my best outfit for the meeting. In short time I was perched at the casement and at liberty to observe Pomeranz through the glass. He was of a type I'd not often seen in my travels, nattily dressed, overweight, and pasty; a man who'd spent very little time outdoors or exercising himself in any way. After some minutes, Walton entered the office and approached the desk; Pomeranz remained seated and declined the handshake. The two appeared to have a testy exchange that came to a standstill before Walton stepped across the room and unlatched the casement. I stepped inside with as much elegance as the manoeuvre allowed. Pomeranz leapt to his feet and skipped clear of the desk – I guessed it the most nimble movement he'd executed in decades; but he ventured no further as I stepped to the center of the room, impeding his passage to the door.

Walton spoke first. "Does this fellow strike you as a poseur, Mr Pomeranz?"

Pomeranz did not answer. I offered my hand.

"This is Franz Frankenstein. Please have the good manner to take his hand."

Pomeranz did not respond except in appearing to release his urine. The smell was unmistakable, though I for one was good-mannered enough to resist a peek at his trousers.

"I assure you he's quite friendly, Mr Pomeranz. He means you no harm."

I pulled the shaded glasses from my chest pocket and put them on. "Might I suggest we sit down?" I said, motioning him to his seat and taking one for myself. The glasses and my voice seemed to have a calming effect; our host sank back behind his desk.

Walton pulled up a third chair. "And so, Mr Pomeranz, what do you think?"

"You have a novelty act, Mr Walton, a circus curiosity. A giant with an unfortunate skin disorder. And blind in both eyes. I have no illusions beyond that."

"Franz, can you please disabuse Mr Pomeranz of his notion of your blindness?"

I removed my glasses, for I could hardly see through the tint, and walked to the bookshelf. There, against all odds, I found *The Sorrows of Werter*. "Goethe," I said, "one of my early favorites." I dried my eyes with my pocket handkerchief, opened the book, and began to read aloud:

In this terrestrial paradise I find that healing balm of troubled minds...The delightful spring expands my heart, and invigorates my frame. All nature rejoices in every tree – in every field – the air is filled with fragrance – the feathered songsters hail the morning, and in the evening Philomel tunes a requiem to the retiring day...

"Enough," cried Pomeranz. "I'll grant that he can see, and he can read. So can we all. The exceptional claim is his emergence from lifeless matter. And, for all the playacting here, that remains ludicrous in the extreme."

"I have the lab notes, Mr Pomeranz. If we were to reach a preliminary understanding, you'd be welcome to review them with your most trusted men of science."

"This has gone far enough, Mr Walton. You've entered my office under false pretenses, and the giant has made an illegal entry through the window. It's time for you both to leave before I summon the constabulary."

"As you wish, Mr Pomeranz. We'll wait to hear from you. And in the meantime, I'd advise you change your trousers. You'll catch your death of cold."

Chapter XV

February 27th, 17—

My Dear Franz:

I have suffered an incident both familiar and novel; another horrible cruelty at the hands of my husband, but in a form I'd not before experienced, nor even imagined. Mr Garvey was on the leave I'd long dreaded; and by the rhythms of our correspondence I judged that a letter from you was due. By a stroke of unexpected good fortune, my husband had not yet seized a letter for his most unwelcome perusal; but he'd made no secret of his increasing agitation at the frequency of your communications; and I may unwisely have worsened his temper by letting slip more indication of my own hostility, and even of defiance, than I would normally allow. In sum, I had ample reason to fear his confiscating the expected delivery. As such, I sat vigilant in my chair, silently agonizing, listening for the sound of the substitute postman and for the movements of my husband about the grounds. At the clack of the postbox door, I judged my husband to be more or less safely in the orchard; and on that basis I left my chair and hobbled immediately to the box. I had just tucked the letter in my skirts — what good fortune to have completed the act! — when the dogs, those vile beasts, bounded into my path, snarling and baring me their teeth, and my husband followed in a hot rage at finding me so near the road. He dragged me across the garden and threw me to the ground, near to the spot where he has killed and hung to bleed many a barnyard denizen for my personal edification. Half expecting such treatment myself, I had the good sense to deny the letter's existence, and still wonder at his not subjecting me to a most barbaric physical search right there in the garden. Instead, in an act beyond all my imaginings, he yanked my boots roughly from my feet. "Enjoy your walkabouts now," he sneered, strode into the house, and cast them into the fire!

As Robert would attest, my boots are not the ordinary sort, but are made especially for someone of my condition, and personalized for me at great effort and expense. Without them my gait goes from simply pitiful, painful and ungainly, to something so hellish in its nature that I can barely abide the spectacle of myself.

The dogs are less taken to the outdoors since the incident, but prefer rather to stalk me in my chair, judging me by my gait, when little I walk, to be some sort of wounded prey. They crouch like two evil sphinxes, one on each side of me. Either in isolation is capable of my slaughter; acting together, the deed would be done within moments. I fear the slightest deviation in my behavior will drive them to it. So beleaguered are my spirits, and so bereft am I of hope, that if I had but the courage, I would willingly bring it on.

I dare write no more for the fear of discovery. As it is, this letter cannot be posted until I can place it in Mr Garvey's kind hands. Please forgive the resulting delay; it is the furthest thing from my want.

Yours very fondly,

Margaret

Since my initial letter to Margaret, and her initial reply, I hadn't shared our correspondence with Walton. He was the model of discretion in that regard, betraying no hint of entitlement on his part, or of obligation on mine. He'd simply hand me the letter if he were the first to retrieve it, and enquire as to Margaret's wellbeing only after some considerate interval, and in a manner that conveyed an implicit trust in my report, and an implicit belief that my small claim to her was no mere novelty, but genuine and altogether proper. This letter, however, raised such an alarm in my mind that I had no choice but to share it at once.

"The monster," he said quietly, folding the pages and handing them back to me. "I'll have another pair of boots made up and deliver them myself without delay. As you've pointed out on more than one occasion, the trip is long overdue. If he gives me more than the usual reason to fear for her, I'll bring her back with me, at the point of a musket, if need be. Your letters, meanwhile, are a danger to her; you must desist in your personal communications."

While the notion of his visit brought me great joy, that of a disruption in our correspondence caused me immediate distress. "I believe she finds much-needed solace in those letters," I said with as much composure as I could summon.

Walton thought for a moment. "Then we'll draft a series of letters from me, suitably dull and executed in your hand; she'll understand to leave one for his discovery in order to defuse his suspicions. Going forward, perhaps you can slip your private paragraphs into the back pages, well beyond the point where a dull-witted man like Saville would bother to read." As I considered it later, his plan, under the circumstances, seemed as good as any.

He was out of the house within the half hour and back an hour later. "It cost me rather a lot," he reported, "but the best man in London is dropping his other work until hers is complete. All credit to her; he's been making her boots since she was a young child, and remembers her fondly on her merits. To this day she thanks him by personal letter for every pair he produces. As such, he promises them for the end of business tomorrow. I'll hire a coach and four to carry me overnight. I sleep well in a coach, and that'll put me at Margaret's door just after breakfast the next day, an arrangement that leaves me at my best advantage. Saville won't willingly have me there overnight, and I'll not need to discompose him by pressing to stay. I'll have had the full day to set her in her boots and to take their full measure; and likewise, for he to take mine."

Chapter XVI

Walton and I spent the next day in a state of agitation, keeping to ourselves and speaking but little. The early meals were desultory affairs. He packed his bag while I tidied up just after noon. His mind wasn't in our chess game, and I had barely the heart to cut down his queen after one particularly careless moment. He must have opened half a dozen books without truly engaging in any of them. Just as he was beginning to despair for the promised delivery, some minutes past 4:30, a courier brought our relief. This time I withdrew to the kitchen until I heard the door latched shut. Walton had made a cursory inspection of the boots, and, satisfied thereupon, had redirected the courier to fetch his coach and four. Now he showed them to me.

"Regular black boots," he said, suddenly reanimated. "Stout, but not altogether uncommon, except for the number of quite clever alterations. The most apparent of these are the metal external buttresses running vertically from the inside of both heels to just under each knee. You can see he's upholstered the interiors to protect her from the cutaneous wounds that kind of rigidity would likely produce. He's also installed new heels with exaggerated leverage to the outside; these combat and control her extreme supination. A slit down the back, a series of clamps and straps, and there you have it. It's a modern wonder, Franz, and a testament to the goodness in man, when so inclined. Imagine the importance of these boots to my sister; and imagine the barbarity of throwing such things into a fire."

"I've prepared you some provisions."

"That's very kind of you. The coach won't be long now. Remember, I should be back the morning after tomorrow. You've got everything you need; there's plenty of food for several days. Just don't leave the house. And don't answer the door for anyone but Pomeranz."

"How will I know if it's Pomeranz without giving myself away?"

"I assumed you'd peek through the curtains. But I suppose you're right; there's too much risk. He's unlikely to call, and if he does you're best not to answer."

"That seems the best course."

The approach of a coach and four is readily known on an otherwise quiet cobbled road. Walton wore his coat and had his bags at the ready by the time the driver rapped at the door. I shook his hand, wished him luck, and retired to the kitchen. I heard him open the door and shut it behind him, and waited for the sound of the coach pulling away. Instead, after some delay, I made out an animated conversation on the stoop. Several people were involved. I snuck into the parlour for a better listen.

"What is the meaning of this?" I heard Walton ask. "I go where I please. What business can it be of yours?"

"You need to stay with us, Mr Walton."

"I'll do no such thing. My invalid sister is in desperate need of these boots. I mean to deliver them."

"You'll have to send them along on their own. Here's the warrant... Hadn't intended to search the house until the morning... We were just meant to keep you at home until then, but the coach changes things, moves up the schedule."

I couldn't make out Walton's rejoinder.

"We're under no obligation to justify the warrant, sir. As a courtesy,

I'll tell you we had a recent complaint from Ave Maria Lane, which we have reason to believe is related to an incident some months past in Drury Lane."

A moment passed without audible comment.

"Please then allow me to make arrangements with the driver."

I bounded up the stairs, and threw my most precious and portable things – Margaret's letters, my glasses, toothbrush, powder and soap – in my sealskin satchel. My thought was to exit through the kitchen; but as the window in my bedchamber looked over the alley, I took a moment to peek through the curtains. Two men stood watch in the dusk. I ran to the next bedchamber, where the window opened not to the front or the rear, but over the adjoining house to the west. I clambered through and managed to shut the window behind me before leaping to the roof below. With my satchel over my shoulder, I worked my way over three rooftops before daring to look back over the street. Two men stood guard on Walton's stoop; beyond the pair in the alley, I knew others were inside with Walton. The driver barked to his team and wielded his whip. The coach jolted into motion.

VOLUME TWO

Chapter I

Had the coach been headed in the opposite direction, I'd have been forced to pass back over Walton's house with the constables there spurred to high vigilance. Instead, it clattered toward me, to the west. I ran with it along the roofline, leaping and climbing as the varying roof heights required, and losing ground with every vertical transposition. It was well past me when I reached the end of the block, at a street too broad to jump. I began an urgent search for the best way down, an awkward chore in fading light.

A word here about my climbing: Walton, like Frankenstein before him, seems to take me for some kind of man-insect, naturally able to scale faces that normal humans wouldn't dare. While I've not challenged him on the point, I would submit that what climbing abilities I possess stem not entirely from my physical makeup; but rather were hard-won, through my early banishment to the alpine wilds, and through despair's reducing effect on fear and pain. I may have certain advantages of reach and strength, but I can assure you there's nothing simple or painless about climbing a sheer mountain face in the dead of winter, any more than there's anything simple or painless about descending four stories on the slim edges of a corner pilaster, as I did in this case.

By now the coach was nearly lost from view, and just cresting an incline. This forced me to a hard run, undesirable for the acceleration of my fatigue, and for the open spectacle of my unnaturally long strides

89

and the rapidity with which I discharged them. The coach's disappearance worried me to greater exertion until I'd finally regained the sight of it. I pulled then to a prudent trailing distance and slowed to the moderate trot that would keep me there. My relief then was redoubled by the preservation of relative quiet on the street; any notice of my person had not galvanized into general alarm or open pursuit.

But I was soon to discover the unhappy difference between stone paving and natural terrain. While the relative smoothness of grade was something to appreciate, the unforgiving nature of each footfall on stone, even in my excellent boots, was unnaturally jarring to my ankles, knees and hips. And until the darkness was full – even afterwards, as I'd learned on Drury Lane – the risks of discovery were overwhelming. A coach and four travels on thoroughfares, not in alleys. We joined one now; other carriages rattled by, and pedestrians dotted the walkways on both sides of the street. I kept to one walkway, kneeling to tie my boots at the approach of pedestrians and running as needed to make up lost ground.

Walton had mentioned arriving by breakfast the next morning, which put something like fourteen hours ahead of me. It figured to more than a hundred miles. I'd done comparable treks, and on much rougher terrain, in pursuit of Frankenstein through Europe; but not after weeks of going soft in the parlour, and not in such concentrated centers of population. I considered boarding the back of the coach, but thought it unlikely I'd go unnoticed, either on my embarkation or at stops along the way. If forced to flee the coach, I'd be hard-pressed to find my way back to Walton's or on to Margaret's; and the former was no longer an option. I resolved then to keep my course, to follow at some distance and hope for the best.

When I judged the darkness sufficient, I abandoned my strategy for avoiding discovery; kneeling and sprinting was not something I could sustain all evening. I have little doubt that several people over those many miles took some portion of my measure, though I never turned to gauge any particular reaction. One thing I knew for certain was that without a horse, none who had seen me could viably engage in my pursuit.

As I loosened to the steadier run, the pounding sensation in my joints relented for an hour or so, but returned then with double the effect. I'd have been in far worse distress had the city not begun to thin out, and the road become dirt. I settled in on that softer, smoother path for another few hours, during which my cravings for water became extreme, and the flesh began to peel from my right heel. Why one heel and not the other? Uneven workmanship on the part of the bootmaker, or on the part of Frankenstein? I know nothing of bootmaking, but I will say this: my creator was undeniably skilled – I often marvel at what he was able to put together – but I do lack the near-perfect symmetry of natural creatures; on close or even middling inspection, parts on one side of my body are imperfectly matched by their counterparts on the other. I considered removing the boots and running without them, but in my softened condition I'd have quickly shred the bottoms of both feet, which I knew from dire experience was the far greater calamity. As the landscape grew hilly, the coach put more distance between us; if not for the carriage lamp I'd have lost it altogether.

Never was a rest so well received as at The Goat & Monacle, an establishment along the main road. Before the coachman had so much as dismounted, I'd veered into the woods to find water. I came upon a brook, and, with as much forbearance as I could summon, tracked it upstream where not befouled with the offal of the inn. There I drank myself into a gasping, bloated stupor. I retained enough sense to move my possessions to a breast pocket, thereby freeing my sealskin satchel to carry water for the next leg of the trip. I settled then near the road to tend my bloodied foot while keeping watch on the coach. The driver had not removed the girths or collars from the horses, a practice I found both lazy and cruel; I'd never left my sledge dogs so encumbered for any extended period of rest. But their discomfort was his convenience; when at some length he returned, he needed only re-apply the bridles and tugs. With a flick of the whip they were again at a trot, and I in a hobble behind them.

I remember little of the next several hours beyond the miseries of my foot and a long string of tormented reflections, thick with regret. What reception, beyond revulsion and hostility, could I reasonably expect at Margaret's? Why had I killed those men in the laneway? Half measures would certainly have sufficed, and I'd now be propped comfortably in my bed rather than running myself half to death. And why hadn't I taken the lab notes from Walton's? They were likely now in the hands of the authorities, all my hopes for a mate thus extinguished. I'd proven a fast and able learner; with those notes I might in time have followed in Frankenstein's footsteps and created a mate, one to my own liking. But surely that was madness; I had no tools or facilities, none of his training, and in all likelihood none of his genius. I might somehow have enlisted the services of a man more learned and capable than I; and yet, murdering the loved ones had not proven a successful approach to motivation.

On occasion I surfaced to more practical concerns, assessing if, in the event of discovery and pursuit, I could still move well enough to escape. The further I dragged along that road, the more clearly the answer was no. If not for the water in the satchel, I'd have been forced to retire. But at last the driver stopped again, this time at a less populated but even louder inn, The Maid & Minstrel, where the men were well into their drink. I reckoned I'd run nearly sixty miles, but judging by the passage of the moon, my journey was only half complete; and it was with this thought that I began to seriously consider commandeering the coach. I'd never driven a team of horses, but I'd had surprising success with my dogs in the north; and having spent most of my life in the wild, I considered myself imbued with a certain empathy for animals, if not with great experience in their handling. The horses had drunk what water the driver had left them; I pumped them out some more, and caressed them as they drank. My dogs had always wanted rubbing at their back hips, but this did not have such a soothing effect on the horses, meaty as they were in that area. Instead, I worked them under their collars, primarily at the pull points at the chest, which I imagined would be well sore. When this had produced its soothing effect on each animal, I took a moment to inspect the coach. The passenger seats held only the parcel with Margaret's boots. But a box nestled under the driver's seat, and running the full length of it, offered a host of tools and supplies, and a packet of maps and manifests. The latter I took the liberty of carrying into the light: clipped atop it was the instruction to Sweetbriar, written in Walton's hand. This decided the matter.

In starting a dog sledge, I would run behind with both hands on the rails, my push supplementing the dogs' pull, and then leap to the runners. Here, I was dead weight. In the far north, the dogs would sense my effort behind them and pull all the more. Here, the horses resented my idle demands. I shook the reins and implored them to move. One of them snorted; the others ignored me entirely. I'd never used a whip on the dogs, and didn't consider it now, stowed though it was just beside me. I jumped down between the rear pair, startling them into action, and with my hands on the crossbar, I pushed right with them. As we picked up speed, I pivoted and flipped myself back over the dashboard. I grabbed at the reins at the same moment that a lurch of the coach jolted me into the seat. This caused an unintended pull; the horses shot hard to the right, and the top-heavy coach swayed distressingly left. On a dog sledge I'd helped to carve the turns, leaning and pressing my feet on the runners, my weight, and that of the sledge, low on the snow. Here I was nothing more than poorly-placed baggage. But we settled in sooner than you might expect, and if anyone had been out to see us, I'm sure we'd have made quite a sight, four strong bays and an overlarge coach thundering down the road, with an ill-begotten eight-foot novice at the helm.

Chapter II

I coaxed the team onto a side lane well before I'd reached the house. It seemed we'd reached Sweetbriar's near edge, and several factors dictated that we go no further. Dawn was upon us, and the coach and I would ill be seen on the road, sparsely traveled though it seemed to be. Moreover, I dared not rattle by the house to awaken its inhabitants, nor to venture upwind of the dogs.

Ample wood on both sides of the lane allowed our easy concealment, and I unhitched the team half a mile in. A quick exploration on foot led me to a canal running parallel to the lane, a quarter mile further west. I led the team to drink, then back to graze near the coach. My own foraging took me somewhat further afoot; winter still held sway, and clearings in the canopy offered the most promising warmer ground. Certainly the sustenance was sparse and unappealing against that to which I'd recently grown accustomed. But I'd known real hunger, desperate hunger, both in my earliest days when I knew nothing of plants and would try all the wrong things, only to retch and lie ill; and also during conditions of deep snow. Despite the heavy toll of the run, even if I'd found nothing, what I'd packed away at Walton's table would hold my strength for some time. But goose grass poked from certain leaf cover, and ale hoof abounded past the shadow of some elders. Holdover acorns lay about, some of them still edible. Beyond that, the coach-box held a modest bag of dried oats meant for the horses. This I was determined to conserve, but I parceled out five small portions by which we supplemented our forage, each horse feeding in turn from my cupped hands – none of them applying so much as a nip, their lips a marvel of gentle dexterity – and I then taking a portion of my own.

In sum, I had but little complaint; and what longing I felt in my stomach, and what pain in my feet, were more than offset by the sun – that glorious morning sun! – streaming through the trees in great yellow-tinted shafts. In the way of most animals, the horses shifted into its warmth without the bother of a look. Having been so long in the dark, I couldn't match their indifference. I tilted my face joyfully and directly into the sun, soaking in its warmth, studying the reddish tint of my own eyelids. I stripped myself to the waist and made several slow turns like a pig on a spit, though the cool wind precluded my continuing for long. Having thus indulged myself, I took to the horses with a grooming brush, honing my technique as their responses demanded, and performing, in the end, quite apparently to their satisfaction. I strung a rope around the trunks of seven trees, forming an irregular hectagon. This acted more as a guideline than a true enclosure; horses with any spirit, and I'd taken this bunch to have that in some abundance, could easily have wandered. But I guessed that they would not; and as each of them lay down in turn, it seemed this would prove correct. I thought to sleep in the coach but found its benches too short and too narrow, and the allure of the sunlight too great; I settled instead between the roots of a great oak.

Only a few hours of that sunlight remained when I finally awoke. It had long since shifted off of me, but my condition was much improved nonetheless. I would feel that run for quite some time, but with the exception of the savaged heel, I was passably functional. The wind had shifted, which turned my thoughts to the dogs; any further shift would bring them presently. The horses were up and grazing; I led them again to the water and back to the coach. There I collected Margaret's boots and returned to the canal, this time to cross it. I carried both her boots and mine as I ventured in, hoping to ford without soaking myself completely. The water rose just above my waist.

With my own boots back on my feet, and Margaret's left near the canal, I proceeded toward the heart of Sweetbriar, coming shortly upon a field that led to a small orchard, and from there to the house. In all probability I needed only to wait, but I stirred the brush nonetheless, with a rustle sufficient to rouse my adversaries on the off chance they required it. Deep braying howls, those reserved, in my experience, for the largest canines, sounded on cue.

From what I've seen of domesticated dogs, they're nothing like their cousins the wolves when it comes to the chase. Well-fed as they tend to be at the hands of humans, they hunt not with the proper urgency for the prize, but with an overriding lust for savagery. They expose their positions far too early, and are then generally outrun or outmaneuvered. There was no guarantee of this in my case, however, so severely did my damaged heel degrade my stride. I had no spring off my right foot, and each spring off the left brought an excruciating landing on the right. The howls grew ever nearer, but I'd spaced things more or less correctly; the nearest dog was still a few bounds behind me when I splashed back into the canal. I had just time to collect myself before it sprung in after me, the second dog just after.

Winded though I was, the scales had now shifted in my favour. They couldn't touch bottom with their snouts in the air, but were forced to swim; I, on the other hand, had the luxury of moving on my feet. I skipped around the lead dog and clamped one hand on each of its back paws. At its immediate endeavours to twist and bite, firm pressure at the ankles realigned its body and returned its jaws to their proper distance. As the free dog approached, I turned the clamped one into its path; and at its every attempt to swim around, I brought their faces back together. Such was their frenzy I wondered they didn't take gouges from each other's snouts. Deranged snarling impeded their breathing and tired them all the faster. A dozen times we did this dance, the free dog making a hard flanking motion, and I swinging the clamped dog to obstruct it. Both were nearly spent, first with the run and now with the struggle in the water. The run had hurt me far more than it had hurt them, but I'd recovered almost fully in the canal, so much more efficient were my movements in the water. One more approach by the free dog; a feint, and then I had it, pinned at the neck under one arm. A hard yank on the remaining back foot, a quick reach, and I'd collared the other with the other arm. Now I had simply to squat to dunk them under, spreading my legs for leverage and mourning my ruined trousers as frantic claws raked the backs of my legs. Sooner than I might have expected, the fight went out of them.

I took no pleasure in those kills — far less, I can assure you, than they'd have taken in tearing me limb from limb. I left their bodies on the bank, where I reclaimed Margaret's boots and headed once more in the direction of the house.

Chapter III

The light was going fast, but not fast enough, as I cut across the field and into the orchard. My plan was to get the boots to Margaret without being seen – I'd tucked a note into the box apologizing for Walton's being indisposed and unable to deliver them in person – and then to monitor Saville's reaction through the windows. If he showed the slightest inclination to destroy the new pair, I would move at once to stop him. I sat with my back to a tree, waiting for darkness and letting my breath go still, listening for any approach by Saville in search of his dogs.

The house was just as Margaret and Walton had described it. If anything, they'd understated the effect of the thorny canopy. It extended two storeys, to the roof-line and beyond; and even in winter one could barely distinguish a wall stone or discern a window through its tangle. When the darkness was such that the indoor lights did manage to shine through, I moved from the orchard through the garden, ruing the shredded pant legs that brushed my calves at every stride. I circled past a shed to the front of the house, where I hoped to see Margaret sitting alone in the kitchen, but could make out only what I took to be her chair.

I continued my loop to the far side of the house. One room was better lit than the others, and I worked through the tangle for a closer look, sustaining still more damage to my clothes and my person. I settled at the casement and peered through the glass; and there by the light of a roaring fire I saw what I can hardly bring myself to describe, so thoroughly did it offend even my sense of propriety, the same that has been variously described as callous, monstrous, and unrefined. A man who could only be Saville, broad of neck and thick of moustache, sat facing me on an upholstered stool. He wore a white shirt unbuttoned at the throat with sleeves rolled above the elbows, dark trousers, and boots. A woman who could only be Margaret lay struggling, face down across his lap, loose hair strewn across her face. She was dressed as no woman I'd seen before, in nothing whatsoever. His burly left forearm, thick with black hair, pressed along the white length of her back, pinning her to his lap. His right hand held a short crop, the type of implement I'd seen used only on horses. He raised it high and brought it down with shocking violence on her naked buttocks. I may or may not have heard the crack of it through the glass; but I heard her scream as if no glass were in place. Her face was a horrible contortion of pain, his a mask of evil delight.

Without so much as a thought, I leapt through the window. My first awareness was of my head and arms passing through the glass. The bottom sill caught me at the knees and tipped me awkwardly as I dropped the several feet into the room, hitting the stone floor with my face and shoulder amid the shards of glass and jagged chunks of wooden framing. Saville leapt to his feet, hurling Margaret like a lap shawl to the floor, and stood for a moment with this mouth agape and his chest heaving as I pulled myself to my feet. Our eyes met and locked in place. "Whoreson devil," he snarled, "I'll see you dead." Then, at an instant, he rushed me with a roar, and I at him. We met like two great mountain rams, cracking straight on. He was the strongest man I'd ever encountered, thick-limbed and taller than he'd looked on the stool. We both reared up, stunned at the collision – I'd now had three of them in rapid succession, with the window, the floor, and the man – and ducked into each other again. This time I had the better of him; I felt his back buckle and his head come up as he reeled on his heels; and I drove him back and down in such a manner that his head cracked loudly on the stone floor. I shifted onto his chest and pinned his arms beneath my knees. The fire poker lay nearby; I tucked it behind his neck and bent both ends upwards, then doubled them across and down until his throat was pinched by a third. I leapt back up, and, to his credit, he leapt right after me, staggering and grasping at his iron cravat and foaming at the lips. I slipped behind him and pulled the poker ends tighter, torquing them until they nearly touched. He dropped to his knees, went purple, straightened, teetered, and collapsed full on his face.

Only now did I look to Margaret. Our eyes met for one long moment, hers in a state of frozen panic. I'd seen eyes that shade of blue only once before – in those of my lead sledge dog, for whom I now recalled a particular affection born of the shared hardships of arduous travel and frigid nights. Margaret broke off this brief reverie, rushing to the door in a jerking, spastic gait that seemed utterly inhuman; it more resembled that of a deer in its death throes, the fatal arrow lodged deep in its chest. I had just time to note the crimson welts that emblazoned her buttocks, and then she was gone. I thought to follow, but returned my attentions instead to Saville, lest he should rise again. This he did not, though he managed in his death throes to flip like a great fish onto his back, the knotted poker clacking sharply on the stone. I watched him through several odd twitches of his feet until at last he lay still. I picked the boot box from the floor debris and set it gently on the table, then dragged Saville from the house by his heels. The two poker ends scratched along the stone and across the threshold; and, though it was too dark to see just then, they plowed a double track in the earth from the door, past the shed, through the garden, out the fence gate, through the orchard, and into the far field. There I let him lie.

I doubled back to the shed, where I was quickly rewarded with a short stack of horse blankets. My clothes were beyond salvaging, I knew; and while they retained some measure of utility, I couldn't bear to abuse them any further. I removed them all, keeping only my boots in place, folded them, and stacked them neatly on the shelf. I fashioned one of the horse blankets in the way I'd often done in the forest, tearing a slot in the center, passing it over my head to drape across my shoulders, and securing the arrangement with a cord around my waist. I took the remaining blankets with me, through the garden, orchard, and field – where I tripped, foolishly enough, on the body I'd just left there – through the woods, across the canal, and under the rope. As I blanketed the horses they smelled the blood on my person, and I was some time in settling them. In the end, two blankets remained for my bedding. I settled back between the two roots of the oak, and held my aching head. I recalled Walton sleeping so strangely on the boat after I'd knocked him about, and now such a cloud settled over me; I dropped to sleep as the rain set in.

Chapter IV

The dawn glowed blood-red as I returned to the field with a limp and a searing headache. I found Saville cold and stiff, with small sections of his face bitten away. I claimed his garments for my own, wishing only that I'd removed them the night before, as they'd taken on some unsavoury fluids. I found them a pitiful substitute for the tailored set I'd left in the shed; but, in testament to his physical stature, they fit better than anything else I'd taken from the backs of men. With the horse blanket atop them, I was tolerably clad.

The better light showed the shed well-appointed with tools and materials; I availed myself of a machete before approaching the main dwelling. Having seen it first by dusk, and now by dawn, I could still discern little of its character beyond the forbidding snarl of its thorny encasement. I hacked my way to the broken window and sat to listen for Margaret. Satisfied that she was still abed, I worked a wheelbarrow to the window and dropped silently inside. I looked at once to the table, gratified to see she'd claimed the boots. I cleared the larger bits of glass and frame through the window, and swept the remnants with the fireplace broom. A large patch of dried blood marked the floor where Saville had struck his head; several smaller patches spattered about were quite as likely mine as his. I wetted them all with a ewer from the mantelpiece, and, finding no alternative, stripped Saville's shirt from my chest to wipe them clean. I left Margaret what sleep remained to her and wheeled away the debris.

I moved then to the field, where I swung a scythe as I'd seen farmers do, cutting a center section of grass neat and low. I raked away the trimmings, and positioned the naked Saville face up in the center of the cleared section. The twisted poker propped his head at a forward angle; this gave him the aspect of observing his own decomposition. I pounded a ring of wooden posts around him, draped a netting to form a porous roof and wall, and secured it at the base of each post. This would keep the birds and larger animals at bay.

Much as Margaret occupied my mind, I would not lurk about and watch without her leave. And I dared not confront her directly for the certainty of terrifying her further. Instead, I busied myself with the preparation of materials to close up the window, a chore I intended for the next morning. I'd never cut a board before, but made do with intuition and a pair of sawhorses much like a pair I'd seen on Walton's ship.

I returned then to the wood to water and brush the horses. My headache worsened as my hunger increased, forcing me to forage immediately thereafter. I was some hours at this, and struggled for satisfaction, fully aware that my exaggerated cravings sprung from the overabundance of plate I'd long indulged at Walton's. I disposed of the dogs, burying them as I'd seen Frankenstein and his party bury his bride, though without the bother of a box. The remaining daylight I spent with my back to a tree, rereading Margaret's letters in the hope of reconciling my dignified and unflappable correspondent with the naked and terrified woman I'd seen lurch from the fire-lit room. The horses seemed to sense my unsettled mood; one of them approached with a quiet snort and a nuzzle I gratefully accepted. I slept but poorly, having grown soft against the hardships of the wood, and fretting over my vision of Margaret.

At first light, I set to boarding the window. By the prior day's measure, Margaret would sleep for some time longer, and I again wished not to disturb her. I found my cuts well-measured, and hammered them into place, with regret at the noise it entailed, but also with a sense of the satisfaction men take from such work. I'd seen that she'd availed herself of all the firewood in that room, which set me to splitting her another load. This I'd done frequently at the cabin I'd once burned, and I hove into it now with violent resolution until the sections lay all about me, like fallen warriors at the feet of a hero. I stacked it thereupon near the kitchen door, where I deemed it most useful for her.

I turned then to the morning's forage, availing myself once again of the modest satisfactions presented in that wintry wood. While certain cravings remained at the end of it, there was consolation in finding myself at liberty for a sit with Saville. I slipped a stool under the net and settled upon it at his feet, his head propped as if to address me directly. Already he was experiencing some changes. His face, unnaturally purple at the time of death, had gone nearly black on account of the flies that crowded onto its surface, and of the ants that swarmed into his eyes, nose, and mouth. His body was naturally hirsute, certainly in comparison to my own, but those patches of flesh not covered with hair, or with insects, seemed oddly loose in their fit, and had taken an odd sheen, as if anointed with foul oil.

Back in the wood, the afternoon light filtered through the canopy. I washed Saville's shirt in the canal to break up the blood-crust; and as his blood and mine ran downstream, so too did his image leave my mind, mercifully replaced by imaginings of Margaret. I read her well-worn letters once more, running my fingers along the creases and tucking them back in their envelopes. I suppose I'd never truly believed we'd be more than fond correspondents. Sophisticated as he was in most respects, an experienced sea-hand like Walton would be rough enough around the edges to stomach my presence; Margaret's sensitivities would be a far cry from his. I'd allowed myself to dream otherwise, most recently during the deepest misery of the run. But now, on the heels of such an introduction – she'd seen me at my murdering worst, raining blood and wreckage into her own home — all such hope was snuffed. I would happily have returned to the role of the unseen correspondent, but fate, I understood, had taken a different turn.

Still, I was happy to have been of some service. I'd seen the boots delivered and the dogs dispatched; and once past the shock of it, she'd appreciate Saville's absence. But there were things he'd provided that she could not provide herself. She couldn't live on goose grass and ale hoof and half-rotted acorns, that I knew. But I could learn the ways of men in these lands, just as I'd learned the ways of Walton's ship, and of his kitchen; and in so doing I could provide for her, establish myself as the benevolent unseen hand. But that kind of learning, gleaned not under Walton's tutelage, but through experimentation and the hidden observation of others, would take time. I assumed some backstores of provisions in her cellar; for now my opportunity, and my obligation, lay in lifting the oppressive darkness of her home, which the boarded window had only made worse.

The next dawn, my third in those woods, brought a chill wind. I pulled Saville's shirt, still as much crimson as cream, from the branch where I'd hung it to dry. I buttoned it up to the chest, the point at which the buttons would no longer reach. My own heat, enhanced by the walk to the canal, passed quickly into that garment, and I felt the return of its better qualities, its subtle retention of warmth and its softness shielding me from the scratch of the blanket. Fording the canal was even more unpleasant than usual in those chill conditions; but nothing to what I'd suffered in the alps and the far north. I held Saville's pants along with my boots overhead, dry things to don on the other side.

Affording Saville but a cursory look as I passed, I continued through the field and orchard and directly into the shed. There I meant to retrieve the machete, but my eye drifted to my clothes, folded on the shelf where I'd left them; something struck me as different, some change in the stacking perhaps, some shift in their order. The pants were still on top; I could hardly bear to unfurl them, disinclined as I was to look upon their many gouges and shredded backsides. But unfurl them I did, and I saw at once that their many tears were mended! And the foul smell and the smears of blood and soil were washed away! A note nestled in their creases dropped to the floor.

March 4th, 17—

Franz:

If you can bring yourself to forego the apparent comfort of the forest, please join me for tea, 3:00 on the 5th.

Yours,

Margaret

Chapter V

Kind as Margaret had been to mend my clothing, her note made plain that I was no longer her *Dear Franz*, but merely *Franz*. And she was no longer *very fondly* mine, or even *fondly* mine, but merely mine, even that but a convention. Those changes confirmed my many lugubrious ruminations. But my heart still sounded like the stride of a cart-horse when I presented at her door, as close as I could put it to 3:00. I hadn't worn my dark glasses since the ill-fated introduction to Pomeranz, but I pulled them on now so as to minimize my reliably horrific effect. At least I was soaped and bathed. My teeth were well-presented; how wretched I'd have been had I not grabbed my brush and powder on the way out of Walton's! And clothing was back in my favor – Margaret had done a better job than I could have imagined with both the stitching and the cleaning, and I'd stripped naked in crossing the canal to keep every article perfectly dry. It was only on the strength of such reflections that I brought myself to knock. She answered at once. On this occasion, clothing was very much in *her* favor. The sun was full upon her, and a black dress set off her fair flesh where it plunged along the lines of her arms and ran across her chest. She took several staggering steps back, but managed not to gasp or to turn away in horror.

"Forgive me," I stammered. "I presume I'm either early or late, as I have no access to a clock."

"Dear God, you're even taller than I thought."

She recovered her manner somewhat, inviting me inside and warning me to mind my head. I maneuvered through the aperture as gracefully as I could, taking small comfort in having surpassed my prior entry in that regard.

"I've often wished to be rid of my own clock," she said, gesturing toward an upright model similar to Walton's. "Ticking away the tiresome days." She spoke more easily when facing away.

"It's a beautiful piece of work nonetheless."

"Not as ornate as my brother's, but it does keep the time. And it shows you to be remarkably prompt; you're set to arrive in twenty minutes."

"Forgive me," I said, turning back toward the door. "I'll return at the appointed hour."

"Don't be silly. Please sit down." Her stride, aided by the boots, was much improved since I'd last seen it, and the taper at her waist showed to great advantage. She motioned to a chair I hadn't noticed before, large and unfinished, with wooden spools fanning up the back. But as she shut the door the house went darker than I might have expected; and despite the weeks behind Walton's thick curtains, I tripped over an unseen ottoman. I caught myself on my hands, straddling the offending piece like a beast on all fours, my glasses clattering on the floor beneath my face.

"Are you alright?"

"Forgive me," I said, scrambling to my feet. We both bent for my glasses, my hand arriving just before hers. "I can barely see through these dark lenses indoors."

"Well, don't put them back on then," she scolded in a cheery sort of way, suddenly looking me straight in the eye with only a hint of blanching, and managing something close to a smile. "And please stop begging my forgiveness." I tucked the glasses into my pocket, and we took our seats. "Do you wear them strictly in the service of vanity?"

"I assure you, Margaret – may I call you Margaret? – vanity is far from any consideration of mine. I meant them only to spare you what unpleasantry I could. I'm told my eyes are my most off-putting feature." I reached instinctively for my handkerchief, thought better of it, then realized I was too far into the motion and went ahead with drying them.

"Are you weeping, Franz?"

"No, but thank you for asking. I'm afraid my eyes run without regard to emotion. They require wiping in the normal course."

"I see."

"I can't thank you enough for washing and mending my clothing. Your brother was most kind to have it made up for me, and I was distraught to have it so horribly used."

"I had no choice in the matter after watching you stack firewood in a toga and short pants. It just wouldn't do."

This was perhaps a bit of humour, much like her brother's.

"I hadn't the notion I was being watched."

"Oh yes, very much so. And thank you in your turn for the firewood, and the window repairs, and for delivering the boots."

"The repairs, I'm afraid, are shoddy at best. And the need for them the result of my own clumsy entrance."

"Clumsy perhaps," she said, looking me full in the eye. "But very much appreciated nonetheless."

I could say nothing, stunned by the penetrating blue of her gaze.

"I'm afraid it all made for a rather sordid introduction," she continued.

"Are you now able to sit in comfort?"

This was the absolute wrong thing to say; I knew it at once. She declined to answer. I could think of no way to put the conversation back on track, but the more I waited, the more awkward my situation.

"I hope I haven't overstepped."

"Do you mean with the impertinent question?" she replied archly, "Or with my unfortunate husband?"

"Either. Both."

"As to my husband, he inflicted enough cruelty over the years to deserve such a fate, and then some. Don't be misled by the black dress – I wear it for your benefit, not for his. Evil as it may be to say, I couldn't be happier to have him gone. I only wish you'd taken a moment to get to know him. You'd have felt all the better for the outcome. I hope you haven't found yourself in a difficult position."

Particularly when seated, Margaret had the grace of a type I'd encountered only once before, in Frankenstein's young bride Elizabeth. In her case I'd not allowed myself the luxury of long admiration lest it jeopardize the fate required of her. But Margaret sat before me now as no woman ever had, more or less composed in the full awareness of my presence, her neck long, her shoulders graceful, her slender arms tapering to delicate wrists and hands.

"I don't recall a position I've enjoyed more than at present."

She made a half smile but granted no reply. We sat then, without words, each passing moment casting further shadow on my manner.

"May I ask how you're finding your boots?"

"They require an adjustment I can't manage on my own, but overall they're performing quite well."

"Might I be of some assistance?"

"Perhaps at some later time."

She stood then to serve the tea, and I leapt up to help as I could. There was bread with butter, and a generous plate of vegetables, lightly roasted.

"This is beyond all expectation, Margaret. Thank you. I've worried about your provisions with your husband incapacitated. It appears I needn't have."

"*Incapacitated* seems an insufficient term for describing my husband, when last I saw him. But, thank you, I'm well provided for at present. The cellar is stocked with flour, sugar, and salt; and with barrels of apples, potatoes and other hardy vegetables. I have a milking cow and laying hens. It's *your* sustenance that would seem the concern. What have you eaten these many days?"

"I'm well-versed in the foods of the forest."

"All the same, I imagine things are a bit sparse this time of year."

"I'm just sorry to have arrived empty-handed."

"I'll grant you that, but only as it pertains to my brother. How is it, Franz, that you've come without him?"

I'd, of course, considered this question in advance. Robert's detainment by the constables would need explaining, so I'd planned to begin with the full account of our disembarkation and the proceedings on Drury Lane. I did so now, though in more detail than I may have intended.

"And you weren't hurt?"

"Only just slightly. Nothing to speak of."

"I'm glad at least of that. So there we have the 'unfortunate incident' Robert mentioned without describing. Please go on."

Over a period of some duration, I described our queries to the publishers, their responses, our visit to Pomeranz, Robert's detainment, and my escape and subsequent journey to Sweetbriar.

"I wonder if he was detained once they'd completed the search," she said at last. "And if so, for how long?"

"I've wondered that myself, and hoped you might provide the answer. I've little experience in the workings of British law."

"Of course." She was still for a moment, presumably contemplating both the fate of her brother and my own ignorance. "In the end," she said at last, "you're the one they're after. I suspect they'll keep him at home for a while, keep an eye on the place in case you come back. Or maybe they'll let him go where he will, following at a distance and hoping he'll lead them to you. Does he, by chance, know you're here?"

"He'd only be guessing."

"And were my letters left behind?"

"No, I have them here."

"All of them?"

"Yes."

"So they can't link me to you directly."

"I don't believe so. Though Robert, of course, was aware of them."

"I doubt he'd share that information. Doing so would compromise me, even if only as a married woman. But from your telling, a few people may have seen you leaving London. And then there's the matter of the stolen coach."

"Yes, I suppose there is."

"Do you think you might return it?"

"I suppose I could."

"As early as tonight?"

"If you think that best."

"I do."

I hadn't mentioned my damaged heel and was loath to now. I reckoned it was sufficiently recovered for walking.

"What's become of the dogs, by the way?"

"Dead and buried."

"Saville?"

"Dead. As I thought you well understood."

"But not buried?"

"No."

"Burnt?"

"No."

"Dumped in the canal?"

"No."

"I'm afraid I'm out of ideas."

"Captain Saville lies in the field."

"In the field."

"Yes."

"Lies there in the open."

"I'm afraid so."

"And you've appropriated his clothing, have you not?"

"Yes, for the purpose of preserving my better things."

"You've wrapped him in a blanket then?"

"I'm afraid not."

"What could possibly be your thought to leave him so exposed?"

This was a question I hadn't considered in advance, though it seems inconceivable now that I hadn't. It occurred to me to now alter the narrative, even just slightly, but an immediate failure of imagination, and something particularly compelling in Margaret's manner, precluded that.

"I am subject to — how shall I say it? — odd inclinations."

"Odd inclinations."

"Yes. Strange longings, if you will."

"Dear God, Franz."

We sat without speaking, and in my case without breathing. The irony was suddenly clear and inescapable; it was not my physical misshapenness that would form the wall between us, but rather my moral depravity, failings of my own making.

"Go on," she said.

"I wish, Margaret, to observe his decomposition."

"Oh. If it's only that…"

"Of course, if you object, I understand completely. I'd be very happy to dispose of him in whatever fashion you'd like."

"No, no. I'd just like to understand your thinking. Is it a matter of simple spite?"

"I think not."

"I would certainly understand if it were. You've been horribly treated."

"In this case, it was you who were horribly treated."

"Thank you."

"To answer your question…if I may borrow the words of my creator…"

"Of course."

"I yearn to see 'the corruption of death succeed to the blooming cheek of life,' to see 'the worm inherit the wonders of the eye and brain.'"

"Ah, yes," she said. "The chronicles of your origin."

"The first small steps."

"I suppose we all seek to understand our beginnings. And I would happily bequeath the body of even my own dear husband to such a pursuit. But won't the forest animals strip him clean well before he reaches the stage you require?"

"I've fashioned a protective enclosure of netting and posts."

"You are a thorough one, Mr Frankenstein!"

"Forgive me."

She said nothing more, but her manner had resumed its former ease. I cleared the tea set, and stoked the fire, then turned my attentions to the clock, which I found in need of winding. She emerged from the kitchen some ten minutes later, bearing two packages.

"I've loaded the boot box with two pieces of appropriately weighted wood and resealed it. If you leave it in the carriage I imagine they're still obliged to deliver it."

"I'm afraid I don't understand."

"Robert told the constables he was shipping my boots – is that not correct?"

"Yes. I heard it directly."

"So if I'm to wear them, there must be some record of their delivery."

"I see."

"It's best to be thorough in these matters."

"I understand. And the other package?"

"Provisions for your journey."

Chapter VI

Just before dark I hitched up the team, addressing each horse in alternating tones of encouragement and apology. They seemed more than willing to stand in for duty, and tolerated my unpracticed hands with admirable grace. Shortly enough we pulled into the lane, headed back along the way we'd come. The several days of rest brought a new lightness to their step; and I too was more comfortable at the reins, from having not just run some sixty miles, and from my increased familiarity with the route, with driving a team, and with the horses themselves. When we passed into more open ground, the moon lay before us to the east, alternately concealed and exposed by clouds moving rapidly from the north. As that heavenly orb was exposed, so too was this humble daemon; at two instances of passing coaches I tamped down the carriage lamp and slumped low in my seat, returning the customary tip of the cap with an understated motion to my own, or, rather, one of Saville's that Margaret had widened to accommodate my head. The miles passed swiftly, and I marked with satisfaction the particulars of the land – undulations in grade, distinctive stands of trees, streams passing beneath us – far better than I had those of the city.

After some hours I pulled onto a side lane to unharness and water the team. For as short a time as I'd known them, parting with these horses at the inn would be harder than parting with my dogs in the far north. The dogs, in that situation, had better prospects on their own;

but the horses, I was convinced, would be better off with me than in pulling for such a careless coachman, at least for as long as I remained on Margaret's estate. The duration of that stay was, of course, the great unknown. Margaret seemed convinced that a constabulary party would appear at some point – in search of me or in search of Saville – a development that in either case could put me on the run. I considered it more likely that she would leave the estate herself, or demand my own departure. As welcoming as she'd been, if things turned out worse than we hoped for her brother, she could well determine that my permanent absence was the only condition of their reunification. None of it made for happy contemplation; and yet the night sky was brilliant to behold, and there was magnificence in my movement beneath it, at the courtesy of such a team, sixteen hooves beating in noble cadence.

The moon was halfway through its passage when I spied The Maid & Minstrel. A small crowd milled outside, and I slowed the team to a walk in hopes of its dispersing before our arrival, which, by the whim of simple good fortune, it did. Thus unobserved did I park the coach where it had stood before; and thus did I unhitch the team and feed and water them, and caress them in turn, and whisper my goodbyes. A bank of clouds wheeled over the moon, and, as if on cue, a group of men swung the inn doors open; I was gone into darkness, striding down the black road to Sweetbriar.

As fast a walking pace as I can maintain, my only chance of beating the sun was to run. But I'd had more than my fill of that, with a heel certain to open on any such provocation. And on this occasion, I'd no coach and four to conceal; dawn, therefore, posed no threat beyond the need to shift off the road at the approach of other travelers. On that basis, I settled into as fine a walk as one could find on this earth, my pace unrushed, my destination a desired one, the path smooth and relatively soft underfoot, the night cool and starry, the moon once again before me, now in the west. My heel proved amenable, my boots somewhat softened from the recent and more rigorous passage. On one hip sat the sealskin with cold drink from the stream; on the other, the provisions packed by Margaret. Such were the pleasures of the journey, it was all I could do to maintain my diligence. Twice, at the sound of horses tardily discerned, I darted into the woods; and once, with time run out, I hurled myself into the tall grass and lay still.

I arrived at Sweetbriar mid-day. Margaret greeted me at her door in a blue muslin dress and mantle. "Well met, noble traveler," she cried. It struck me as vaguely Shakespearean, but I could offer no comparable reply, though I'd spend much of the day wracking my brains for one. A fine meal awaited me nonetheless, and a letter from her brother, which she read aloud.

To Mrs Saville

March 4th, 17—

My Dear Sister:

I trust that your boots have arrived, and apologize for their doing so without my personal accompaniment. You may find this beyond the limits of belief, but in the very act of boarding the coach with boots in hand — boots that Stephens produced, quite heroically, in a single day — I was suddenly detained by a considerable team of London's most redoubtable constables!

By way of background, I should explain that the incident transpiring on Drury Lane, the one I mentioned in an earlier letter, was a late-night donnybrook as short in duration as long in consequence, that being the unfortunate deaths of two men, despicable alley sots though they were. On that basis, the constables were in search of Franz, and had apparently been posted at my house for some time. They now questioned me quite aggressively, while also taking it upon themselves to search the premises. I did not dissemble for even a moment, but freely admitted my presence on the occasion in question, corroborating the causes of death while insisting, as is wholly the truth, that Franz acted only in self-defense when surrounded and assaulted by a drunken mob. Nor did I deny that I'd harboured him for some period following, as had been my intent prior to the incident. Indeed, the search produced, among other evidence of his presence, clothing in sizes far too large to be passed off in any other way. But the search failed to produce one critical component — Franz himself! I refused to answer as to when I'd seen him last; for this and other failures in the service of justice, primary among them my not coming voluntarily forward, I was taken into custody, and held for three nights! Only after long effort on his part, and great expense on mine, could my attorney secure my release, which occurred but this morning; and even now I am a prisoner in my own home, constables stationed front and rear.

As I made abundantly clear to the authorities, I have no idea as to Franz's whereabouts. It is in my nature to worry, but he is a resourceful fellow, albeit poorly acclimated to the city. My great hope is that he stays well clear of this place until I've secured his proper scientific reception, and with it the protection he so rightly deserves, and so evidently requires.

As I also made clear, I have no illusion of a fair trial for Franz were he to be apprehended, this being due to his appearance and his origin, and to the great public spectacle such a trial would engender. That said, the authorities have given my account of his origin no more credence than have the publishers, the relation of whose unprofessional behavior would require a lengthy telling in itself. Suffice it to say that none of them has embraced the historic science in question; and one of them, a fatuous ass by the name of Pomeranz, has been the principle agitator linking Franz to Drury Lane, while having the audacity to threaten me directly with civil action! I initially feared the authorities might retain the manuscript indefinitely, but they showed remarkably little interest after their first cursory look; and, in fact, seem to consider me a kind of lunatic on its account, which may, ironically enough, have played a helpful role in my eventual release. And yet, for all their sneering dismissals, those same authorities have determined it prudent to keep these developments from the public eye!

On that note, and in closing, I would strongly encourage you to keep these same developments unknown to your cur of a husband, if he hasn't, heaven forbid, already intercepted this letter. Among other things, the threat of my retribution to his person must be kept intact — as it would not if my house arrest were known to him — in the event of his destroying the new boots as he did the others, or of his inflicting any further cruelties on your gentle person. My thoughts are ever with you.

Your affectionate brother,

Robert Walton

"What exactly is meant by 'taken into custody?'"

"Generally, it would entail being locked in a cell."

"I've not had that experience. But Frankenstein described his own such detainment quite unfavourably."

"I'm sure Robert has emerged with little scarring. He always does. The good news is that if he suspects you're here, he doesn't betray it. And given the uncertain date of your departure from the constabulary point of view, your following the coach would seem a less likely suspicion. I'll hold my return letter until the boot box is delivered, which I expect in the next day or two. Surely the coach and four are recovered by now."

"I would hope so, for the sake of the horses."

"Speaking of which, we have horses of our own here. You would do me a great service to look in on them. I've managed it just once since your arrival. The stables are down the westbound path, if you haven't already come across them."

"I'll do that now."

"And then, I suspect, you'll be in need of some sleep."

"Yes, I may spend the afternoon accordingly, unless you have other pressing needs. In the morning I thought I might begin to clear the overgrowth from the house, if that is still your wish."

"That would be wonderful, Franz." She sat for a moment saying nothing, relishing, I believe, the prospect of domestic sunlight. "You seem to begin your activities earlier than I'm about," she said at last, "so I'll leave a breakfast for you in the shed. There's no need to forage here, unless you find that the flavours of the wood exceed my own."

"I assure you they do not, and I thank you for your troubles."

"And when you begin the work, do so in the rear. You don't want to be seen in front by the coach driver or the postman." The house was protected from the road by a high hedge, but cuts for the drive and the walking entry, both of which were lightly gated, provided threatening sightlines. "I've a bell on both front gates; when you hear one, you'll know to conceal yourself."

While the barn for the other animals stood within Margaret's walking range, the stables were too removed for the consistent application of her personal care. My visit, as she'd indicated, was thus overdue. The residents were unambiguous in their strong dislike of my person; but as they were somewhat desperate with thirst, my presentation of water earned me a degree of tolerance. I judged the air to be foul, and the bedding long unchanged; and once I'd opened the stable doors wide, both horses conveyed a yearning to be out, and, against their better instincts, suffered me to lead them. They were a matched black pair, both mares, and sleeker than the four bays I'd just delivered to The Maid & Minstrel, built more to the run than the pull. I left them to graze in the front garden, where the fresh grass, sparse as it was, seemed an unaccustomed indulgence for them, and the view of them an unaccustomed indulgence for Margaret, who sat with a sanguine expression near the open door.

On my way to the wood, I sat another turn with Saville. His presentation had declined markedly. Such was the scent he now exuded,

I was obliged to bunch a cloth across my face and knot it at my neck; only with that in place could I make the proper inspection. The larger share of the blood he'd not spilled on the parlour floor had settled quite decisively within his person, giving that part of him furthest from the ground a pale green, vacant hue, and that nearest it an aspect of angry red; a smaller share, however, was forcing its own rude exit, as evidenced by the red-tinted foam issuing from his mouth and nose, and quite possibly from between his buttocks, though my inspection there was limited to a cursory lift of the leg. Maggots bunched in those same orifices, and in the eyes, which had burst like rotted eggs, and in masses beneath the skin. And most extraordinarily, while a stout man to begin with, Saville seemed to have doubled in girth, bloated like an over-stuffed bladder in every aspect of his body, his fingers and toes little pork sausages, his arms and legs great rotting hams, his abdomen a great sack of mead. At particular stress points I detected splittings of the skin I deduced were but preliminary in nature.

All this duly noted, I returned to my camp, where, with the rope enclosure taken up, and the carriage and horses returned, nothing awaited me but my satchel, half a dozen blankets, and Saville's filthy clothing. I shifted these to Margaret's side of the canal, where I found a new pair of suitable roots and curled up between them.

Chapter VII

First light found me crawling on my belly, worming myself beneath the thorny tangles in pursuit of the great trunks from which they issued. One blanket formed a great cloak trailing from my head; another, tied at the waist, formed an apron over the back of my legs. This was sufficient to blunt the tearing such a thorny network would otherwise have inflicted on my flesh, but not sufficient to eliminate it entirely. I bled freely about the hands and wrists, and, I suspected, from assorted gouges beneath the blankets. But progress was marked, and immensely satisfying.

When I reached a trunk – inevitably in close proximity to the house, and thereby requiring the longest crawl – I would lift myself, thorns pressing themselves most convincingly then through my blankets, to enable full strokes of the blade; and having hacked clean through, I'd tie a rope in place and reverse myself to exit. Back on my feet, a series of hard tugs on the line would pull a whole section clear, and I'd drag it away directly, through the orchard and into the field where Saville lay. By late morning, the pile was expansive in area and well taller than I, and the rear wall was handsomely cleared. The newly exposed stones showed themselves surprisingly pleasing, both in cut and in application, with appealing detail around the windows and doors. Margaret threw open each of the casements, leaning into the sun and exclaiming in wonder at the light that poured inside.

Toward mid-day came the pounding of hooves and the ring of the bell, and she scurried off to meet the coachman with his precious delivery of two sticks for the fire. I had a mind to circle around and consort with the bays, but knew it to be reckless behavior, certain to meet with Margaret's disapproval, and I banished it from my mind. The time was insufficient in any case; they started presently away. Before the hoof-beats had grown faint, Margaret approached with the package in hand, pleased with her ruse.

"You're bleeding!" she exclaimed, and took my hands in hers for closer inspection. No one, man or woman, had ever touched me in such a fashion while I lived and breathed; I stiffened for a moment, but did not withdraw. She insisted I follow her in. We stood at the basin, where she took my hands once more, washed them and applied a salve.

"Saville would have leather gloves in the barn, but I'd place little hope on their fit."

"His boots were much too small, if that's any indication."

"Then let me wrap your hands. Or better yet, why not leave off for the day? Have your bath, and I'll prepare a meal."

I chose the wrap, more for the novelty and great appeal of her ministrations than the urgency of the work, though I did harbour some eagerness to complete a second face of the house. She had strips of rolled cotton – generally intended, she said, for horses' ankles – and with these she wrapped my hands in a skillful manner so as to maintain the movement in my thumbs. We'd agreed to take tea later in the day, but, as it happened, remained in each other's promixity for most of the intervening period. I began my attack on the east wall; and she, seeming to enjoy the outdoors and the spectacle of her house being emancipated in sections, alternated between scrubbing the stone with a bucket and brush, and sitting in a chair I'd set in the garden, watching and writing in turns. One of the mares took sport in positioning herself directly before Margaret, blocking her view in a demand for caresses, and quickly returning when shooed away.

"What a difference!" she'd say when not engaged with the mare or her writing. Or, "that's a great lot," as I'd tug a section clear and haul it past her toward the field. "I see you're leaving a few select plants."

"I'd be happy to remove them all if you wish, but I'm loath to make things too bare. The ones I've kept bear no thorns, and, while stunted at present, should grow full with steady sun. I'm hoping they'll provide a certain cheer, and a softening effect, while stealing no light from the interior."

"I heartily approve. Now pull up a chair; I've written my answer to Robert, and would have you read it before posting."

To Mr Walton

March 7ᵗʰ, 17—

My Dear Robert:

I've taken delivery of the boots just this morning, several days later than you must have expected. The driver had the most extraordinary explanation; either he takes me for a great fool, or such events really do occur in our age. As he told it, he and the boots were well on the way here on the evening of the 1ˢᵗ, when he stopped at The Maid & Minstrel for a hot bite and a pint — just one, he was quick to assure me — and upon his return to his coach and four, determined them to have departed without him! Some five days later, he had notice of their return, exactly where he'd left them, the horses in as fine or better condition than before, and my boots on the very same seat.

And yet, it would seem that this is not the most extraordinary event in our respective weeks! I am flabbergasted, almost beyond words, to hear of your detainment! As a gentleman who has certainly committed no crime, a man of philosophy and science, an explorer enduring untold hardships in the cause of the greater good! — you are certainly ill-used. And for three long nights! (Though

I imagine you've spent time as dreary in any number of godforsaken ports and in grey, pitching seas.)

As to Franz, my heart is twice broken; that once again he is set upon by a brutish mob, through no provocation of his own, and daemonized for defending himself as any man would; and that, even as I write, he slinks about the streets of London, scraping for his sustenance by night, and hiding like a hunted animal by day, unjustly deprived of the company and protection of his only benefactor in all the world. My assumption as to his whereabouts, however, is of course but a guess, and with any luck a bad one. I, like you, am prone to worry, to imagine the worst; but I take comfort from your assurance that Franz is nothing if not resourceful. Perhaps he has stowed aboard to France, and from there travelled by foot to the lands of his origin; those being, in all likelihood, the lands he loves most, or dislikes least. Please do keep me abreast of any news you may have of him.

Rest assured that the boots are being put to immediate and rigorous application, and all thanks, once again, to you, and to Stephens, whom I shall address in separate correspondence.

Your affectionate sister,

Margaret

"My presence here is inadmissible, even to your brother?"

"The authorities are almost certainly opening his mail. The letter is meant for them."

"But how will he know the truth?"

"Not by my hand, surely."

"Perhaps he'll make a visit."

"Not for some time, if he at all suspects your whereabouts. He'll not willingly lead them here. And even without such suspicion, he'd be unlikely to arrive soon. Sweetbriar has never been a favoured destination for him. Now go wash up, and I'll set the tea."

"I mean to clean the stables first, but it shouldn't long detain me."

I propped the doors to admit fresh air, then, as I'd seen farmers do, mucked out the badly soiled bedding with the lively use of a pitchfork, and spread clean straw in its place. On my way out, my attentions turned briefly to a carriage sitting idly in the corner. I know it now to be a curricle, a two-wheeled chaise, nothing like the coach I'd driven to and from The Maid & Minstrel. It held a seat for the driver and for someone beside him, a retractable shade, and nothing more. While light enough for a single horse to haul with ease, it was rigged for two, offering the promise of a spirited ride.

No sooner had I returned to the house, washed and dressed for tea, than Margaret inspected my hands and applied a fresh coat of salve.

"If you begin again early tomorrow, you'll need to wrap these yourself. Do you think you can manage?"

She handed me a clean cotton strip and had me make several attempts until I'd shown tolerable competence.

"I'll leave clean wraps in the shed with your breakfast."

"You are too kind. And you must let me prepare the next meal," I said, noting the spread of vegetables, lightly roasted, with boiled eggs, bread and curds.

"I've read Robert's fine reviews of your cooking. And I do look forward to partaking. But for now, if you've no objection, I'm better served with you doing the work that I'm least suited or least inclined to do. Have you ever milked a cow?"

I owned that I had not.

"Tomorrow then, if you can break from your clearing, I'll instruct you in that time-honoured practice."

"I look forward to it, though you mustn't detain me for long. I'm determined to finish the clearing."

"I can't thank you enough. Even now, the house is utterly transformed. I imagine you've quite a pile in the field."

"I expect to double it tomorrow. Do you enjoy a bonfire? When it's complete, I thought we might put the torch to it."

"And to Saville along with it?"

I didn't immediately respond.

"He's been out there the better part of a week. I know very little of his affairs outside of the home, but if he's missed somewhere, we may well have an inquiry. His decaying body, set in a cage with an iron about the neck, would be difficult to explain. Have you, to this point, had any satisfaction with – how did you put it? – death's succession and the inheritance of the worm?"

"Some, yes. It remains a work in progress."

"Would a few more days be sufficient?"

"I believe it might."

"Let's plan on that then."

After tea, Margaret showed me through the library, a cozy room newly sunlit from one side. While not nearly as extensive as her brother's, it held a complete set of well-thumbed Shakespeares, Margaret's personal favourites, and another few dozen assorted volumes.

"Which of the Shakespeares do you most prefer?"

"The comedies," she said at once.

"But the most renowned works are the tragedies, are they not? Hamlet, Macbeth, Romeo and Juliet, Othello, Lear..."

"Overly grim, the lot of them. Teeming with deception, murder, and death. I've marked the most brilliant speeches, and regularly take the time to admire them. But I much prefer to inhabit the comedies. Teeming with deception, love, and magic."

I excused myself at the first sign of dusk to return the mares to the stable. I watered and brushed them, and let them enjoy the fresh hay and improved air. Half an hour later, we pulled in front of the house in full harness. Margaret met me with a lamp and a look of disbelief.

"Put on something warm, Margaret. The stars are revealing themselves, and are best seen from the seat of a lively carriage."

"I haven't been on a carriage in ages, Franz."

"All the more reason to do so now."

She grabbed her cloak, and I lifted her to her seat. These mares were prancers by nature, compared to the bays I'd borrowed from The Maid & Minstrel. The weight of the curricle was as nothing; and having stood idle too long, they stamped and huffed at the happy prospect of an evening run. And so it was that we entered the road at a canter, the exhilarating three-beat gait I'd never experienced as a driver. It would be an exaggeration to claim I was actually driving, though I'd have managed to slow them if Margaret had shown any sign of discomfort. But the look on her face, as best I could judge it with quick glances in the coming dark, was one of pure elation; she grasped my arm and uttered little exclamations of delight. The springs seemed in good repair, and the road in fine condition for the season; rather than being shaken as a penance for our speed, we found ourselves rewarded with the bracing breeze and the rapid passing of blackening trees, with scattered clouds on the move and stationary stars beyond them, and with the easy bliss of weightless passage.

Afterwards, I stoked the fire and Margaret poured tea. We were happily spent from the exertions of the day and the exhilaration of the ride. Margaret rocked softly in her chair, cupping her mug with both hands and saying little, though, uncharacteristically, I had no inclination that I was failing her in conversation.

"If you wouldn't mind, you could help me off with my boots," she said of a sudden. I looked to her for further instruction; she held my eye and began to lift her skirts. "And while we're at it, this is probably as good a time as any to make the adjustments. I expect you'll be preoccupied in the morning."

I hesitated for a moment, unclear as to her direction, uncertain as to my duty. But at length I took my cue and knelt before her, feeling my breath go short and my heart to a gallop. She commenced with a series of soft commands, guiding me through a sequence of adjustments, the shiftings of metal buttresses, the reapplication of a leather straps. These I managed despite a certain unsteadiness of hand. She stood and walked a few paces to assess my work, then resumed her seat and guided me through removing the boots entirely. I found myself grasping her stockinged feet, curled under like tender, wounded paws, and kneading them ever so gently between my thumbs and fingers, as I had on occasion the paws of my sledge dogs.

"Tell me Franz, had I not left the note, how long did you intend to remain a stranger in the wood?"

My hands stopped as if on their own volition; I searched for the answer most likely to please while willing them back into motion. But once again, her manner compelled a candid response.

"Indefinitely," I said, with composure that surprised even myself.

"I thought as much."

"Do you think the less of me for it?"

"Not at all, Franz. Not at all."

Chapter VIII

Forming the pyre, in the end, was as much work as the cutting and hauling. Certainly I'd spent more time than expected, and suffered an equivalent toll in the accumulation of cuts and gouges on my flesh. I'd used a pair of long stout staffs to press the thinner vine into several barbed balls, each as tall as I. These I'd rolled tightly together, and atop them I'd stacked the thicker sections, painstakingly sawn to length. I'd added deadwood from the long-neglected orchard until the pile, though well-compressed, was twice my height. Finally, I'd disassembled Saville's netted ring, and with the help of a stepladder, laid its posts in a cross-hatched pattern atop the pyre. This formed a relatively flat, slatted surface; there Saville would lie to burn.

The field lay beyond Margaret's walking range. I'd brought her by the curricle; but wary of the horses' reaction to both the corpse and the fire, I'd hauled it myself, with the pull pad tucked under my arms and across my chest. She was resplendent in her black dress, and I in my finest, as we pulled the cloths over our faces, knotted them at our necks, and approached the body on foot. We took positions, side by side. With the netting removed, our view was unimpeded. She'd been surprisingly eager for this final look at her husband, and he proved more than worthy of her anticipation. His limbs, much as I'd last seen them, were puffed like gigantic sausages, the iron cravat engulfed and nearly lost from view; but such bloat had proven unsustainable at the midsection, where he'd split just left of center and delivered a pool of putrefaction into the surrounding grass, which now lay flat, slick and discoloured. His own hue was mottled with the uneven drainage of his blood and the larval clustering just beneath his flesh; but in general terms it had shifted from the predominant green I'd last seen to a deep crimson moving quickly to black. The hair on his body was slick and matted to his flesh. His eyes were simple portals to the skull, where odious movement suggested a thriving population within. As Margaret and I admired these wonders, hints of orange, pink, and purple tinted the western horizon, and her gentle hand took mine. This was a gesture wholly unexpected. The fluids came rapidly to my eyes; I reached awkwardly across my body, seeking my pocket kerchief with my off-hand.

Only after some minutes, spent mostly in silent wonder, could I bring my hand to disengage. I rolled Saville into a horse blanket, and heaved him – with a bit of difficulty that sent a spurt of putrid fluid onto my jacket – onto his back atop the pyre. The blanket came partly undone, and his arms fell away to the sides, leaving him exposed to the sky in a manner Margaret thought particularly theatrical. In addition, his head hung just off the pyre to our side, his mouth agape and his once-proud moustache matted and slimed, nearly indistinguishable from the rest of his rotting face.

Dusk fell over the land. To Margaret lay the honour of the light, a duty she discharged with steady hand. The fire cracked to life, and we took several steps back as it heated and surged from one edge of the pyre to the other. Flames leapt past Saville toward the sky. We removed our facecloths and happily filled our lungs with the scent of woodfire, and of charring flesh. I pulled the curricle into its most advantageous position, and, once I'd stripped the offensive jacket – Margaret commented quite wryly that "Saville didn't smell much better when he was alive" – we wrapped ourselves in blankets and enjoyed the blaze on its well-cushioned seat. I retracted the shade; the vista from that field was as broad as any I'd enjoyed since the arctic – and of course, I'd been too miserable there to pay it proper heed. Among the whooshing air and crackling wood now came a series of gurgling pops, as certain body cavities, already strained beyond their anatomical limits, bubbled and burst. I'd selected, and with some effort memorized, a suitable passage, and thought this the time for its delivery:

> *Ill-weav'd ambition, how much art thou shrunk!*
> *When that this body did contain a spirit,*
> *A kingdom for it was too small a bound;*
> *But now two paces of the vilest earth*
> *Is room enough.*

"Is that the Prince, Franz? Henry IV, Part I?"

"The same."

"A lovely speech, and well-recalled. But not perfectly suited here, with Saville burnt and not buried."

"I'm afraid I don't understand."

"'Two paces of the vilest earth' – it refers to a grave."

"Oh, I see. More appropriate for your dogs then."

"I suppose so. Though I never credited them much for ambition."

"What little they had was certainly ill-weav'd."

"I'll grant you that."

"Shall we dig them up in the morning?"

"No, Franz."

We slipped into silence. The fire crackled, and the night beyond it went dark and cold. The stars glittered all about, embers rising as if to join them. Margaret's hand was once again a smooth, cool wonder in my own. Presently the cross-hatched platform burned through, and Saville thumped to the coal bed beneath. There he hissed and spit unseen.

Some hours later, with the fire mostly spent, I wheeled Margaret back to the house. She insisted on washing all of my clothes at once, bidding me to stoke the fire and set the water pots, and then to remove the offending garments. She turned gracefully away as I slipped into Saville's gown, which fit only slightly better than had Walton's. I imagined its effect to be equally comic, but she made no such indication. I watched her slender arms at work, wonders of graceful movement, as she washed each piece and ran it through the rollers. When she'd finished wringing and had hung the clothes to dry, she had me fill the tub and motioned for me to step in. I removed the robe and, too late, realized that this time she hadn't turned away, but rather stared quite directly.

"My God, you make Saville look like a gerbil."

I could think of no response.

"I'm glad to see," she continued, "that Frankenstein had at least some humour about him."

"You refer to my appendage?"

"I do."

"I noticed you've none whatsoever."

"Pardon me?"

"I noticed you've no appendage."

"You noticed that."

"Yes."

She had the look of being suddenly quite perplexed.

"You don't quite understand these things, do you?"

"Robert educated me somewhat. I noticed his was on the small side as well."

"I'll thank you not to discuss my brother in that regard."

"Forgive me."

I dipped into the water. We said little more. I soaped and brushed, and Margaret very kindly added two pots of hot water.

"May I prepare the tub for you?" I asked when I'd dried and re-claimed the robe.

"Perhaps at some other time," she said with a smile. "But you may sleep in Saville's bed tonight. Your clothes are much too wet for venturing out."

And so it was that I spent my first night within the walls of Sweetbriar. I'd left my toothbrush and powder in the wood, but Saville's sufficed. As at Walton's, I had a short bed, and a side table, a candle, and a leatherbound Shakespeare – a comedy, on Margaret's recommendation. I recall admiring one line at one moment –*"Hereafter, in a better world than this, I shall desire more love and knowledge of you"* – and morning at the next. Saville's room opened to the east, and the sun was upon me at its earliest inkling. Margaret's opened to the west; this explained her ability to sleep well past first light. But I suspected that before my labours, little sun had suffused any of the casements, north, south, east or west.

Chapter IX

Had I still been foraging, I'd have delighted that the better season was nearly upon us. Dandelion, watercress, nettles, chickweed – already these abounded; and it was all I could do not to crush any of a half dozen mushroom varieties underfoot. But to Margaret's thinking, I was not to fritter my time on such measly fare. There was plowing and planting to be done, the intricacies of which I knew little, and Margaret little more. But she pulled farming pamphlets from the cellar; these she read by candlelight, and carried in the curricle, where she sat for some time each day to observe my work. With two of us so engaged, our errors were quickly amended, and our successes redoubled.

The mares were displeased to be put to the plow, but were goaded to consent, and in the end, comported themselves admirably. I removed hundreds of stones – Saville's hired hands had been deficient that way over a period of many years – and stacked them with a mind to later replicating some of the stone walls I'd so admired in those lands. At Margaret's request, that stack rose directly over Saville's remains. The skeleton had not burned away, as we'd foolishly hoped, but held curiously intact, and relatively clean but for some small bits of charred sinew. The iron cravat stayed neatly in place, projecting, in combination with the bared and slightly upturned teeth, a surprisingly rakish air. Margaret was unwilling to bury those bones in the earth, wanting nothing like a fresh grave in the event of an official inquiry. And they resisted my spirited attempts to crush them with stone. I was able to crack and ultimately to flatten the skull, but on the whole, their resilience was remarkable. So I piled the stones directly atop them until the mound was quite formidable; exposing those bones would take a more determined effort than any constable's hunch would inspire.

To Mrs Saville

March 10th, 17—

My Dear Sister:

The tale of your boots is as strange on your end as on mine. But as it resolved happily, with their ultimate presentation to your person, I shan't belabour its mysteries, which I fear shall never be known to us.

My own story, I'm afraid, remains a bleak one. Despite our daily protestations, and the legal expenses that accrue on their account, I remain under house arrest. My attorney advises me that the arrangement hangs in a daily balance, and could resolve itself as early as tomorrow, or as late as next week. But for now, beyond the constables posted front and rear, he himself makes up my only company; and given the accumulation of his hourly charges I am ever desperate for his removal.

None of the publishers have thought the better of their ill-considered responses. On that score I suppose I should be content that Pomeranz has not proceeded with his civil action; though I find my thoughts turning now to the increasingly well-regarded scientific cadre in Edinburgh, which may prove a more open-minded crew than the stuffed shirts here in London. The entire enterprise, of course, depends on the return of Franz, and — alas! — I have no word of him, either through direct correspondence, or through general reports of any sightings. I am convinced by now that he has quitted London — such a prolonged concealment would be otherwise impossible — and, as you suggest, has found passage to Europe. I fear that he will not write for fear of revealing his whereabouts, and that I am to hear no more of him. In such event, I will have failed him, and my dear friend Frankenstein, and the noble advancement of science, while destroying my own humble fortunes in the same broad stroke.

Your affectionate brother,

Robert Walton

"His letters tend overly to the dramatic," Margaret said, placing the pages face down on the table.

"He does seem more even-keeled in person."

"Your influence was beneficial. And a fine nautical expression, by the way, even-keeled. Did you acquire many such expressions in your time at sea?"

"Only what I learned from Walton. I had not a word from anyone else. Certainly I'm full to the gunwales after the feast you've just presented."

"Hah, was that a shot across the bow?"

"I believe it was."

"Feeling a bit broad in the beam, are you?"

"I'm a loose cannon, Margaret. You'd best batten down the hatches."

"I imagine the latter to be Robert's favorite command," she said, her face suddenly shedding its good humour. "In your estimation, did his tangible lack of courage contribute to the insurrection of the crew?"

"I couldn't say, Margaret. That all happened before I took residence on the ship. And from that point I was ensconced below decks. But I never knew him to lack courage."

"And yet it was Frankenstein, on the verge of death, who was obliged to argue his case."

"So it was written."

"Tell me, did Robert come to your aid on Drury Lane?"

"I never considered it. It all happened so quickly. I know he pulled me away before things got any worse."

"But you don't recall his confronting any of your attackers directly?"

"No."

"I can tell you that he cowered like a rabbit before Saville, from their first meeting to their last. He never lifted a finger on my behalf, with Saville, or with my father before him."

"I'm sorry to hear that, Margaret."

She declined to reply.

"I suppose we all have our limitations."

Again she made no answer.

"I must remind you I was of no aid to Walton when the constables took him. I fled the scene, which is something he didn't do on Drury Lane."

"The comparison has no merit. You had no idea when you fled that they would take him; only the certainty that they would take you, and that he was aligned with you in wishing to avoid that. He wasn't being attacked; nor was he in the slightest danger of being attacked. Nor was there any chance of his ever really escaping them; if you'd helped him elude them on his stoop, where was he to go, and what was he to do? He's not suited, nor the least bit inclined, for the fugitive kind of life you've led. In the end he spent a few nights in prison, an inconvenience and a humbling certainly, but nothing for you to have lost your life over. Those constables would have killed you on the spot or taken you in to be hung. And Walton, by his own reckoning, would be much the worse for it."

Chapter X

Our crops took hold, a wonder beyond most anything I'd experienced on this earth. Every delicate sprout was as surprising and exhilarating as the next; I'd have defended each of them to the death. As it happened, sun and rain took centre stage in favourable cadence, and I played but a minor role, supporting certain plants with stakes and trellises, poking at the edges to keep the soil supple, plucking out leafy intruders, and patrolling on moonlit evenings to frighten away all manner of rodentia. Much of the crop came early – the lettuces, beans, peas, and others – providing most welcome additions at table to the stores from Margaret's cellar, all of which were nearing the ends of their useful lives. Other varieties, half-formed, winked from their earthy beds, hinting at delights to come.

Sweetbriar meant the glorious outdoors, and the freedom to make my mark in it. Spared its natural discomforts by the shelter of a stout and well-appointed house, I could revel in it all the more. With the field successfully under cultivation, other projects laid claim to my devotions. The orchard required more pruning, and the hayfield the removal of shrubs that had encroached for years, many of them as tall as I. The paddock called for expansion, being far too small for the animals we kept; they chewed the grass to the nub, and their hooves, patrolling the same worn paths, turned them quickly to mud. Adjoining land was ripe for the taking; it required only fencing. Accordingly, I began to cut straight saplings near the canal, where they grew too tightly in any event; to haul; to cut them to length and shape; to sink the posts; and to fasten the cross beams.

For all our abundance of cows and sheep, we both had a revulsion for the slaughter of such peaceful beasts, and Margaret as little interest in the meat as I. The animals grazed with a new expectation of longevity, and the forest flavours I brought to table were all the more welcome on that account, as garnishes, salad additions, or courses unto themselves. We had eggs, milk, butter, and curds; and Margaret was progressing with her cheeses.

As to life in the home, I had the same comforts I'd enjoyed at Walton's — warming fires, a roof over my head, a soft clean bed, a room of my own. The library wasn't as large, or the food as extravagant, but both were well beyond sufficient; rather, they were great luxuries I would never fail to appreciate. Margaret and I played no games and prepared no manuscript. But we read aloud by evenings' fires, something I'd not done with Walton; and we worked together in many areas of domestic life, as partners rather than as master and clerk.

The greatest improvement in my station was Margaret herself. She was less remote and more engaging than her brother, much as he remained dear in my memory, and with not nearly the effort he'd seemed required to expend. My learning felt as robust as it had under Walton, but the lessons not the least bit dogmatic; I hardly knew they'd occurred until I'd walked away from some spirited conversation or some entirely natural activity with a new understanding of humanity and the greater world. It was an education less of instruction than of shared experience and mutual discovery, though even the slightest bit of reflection would reveal her to be the guiding force on every occasion.

And unlike with Walton, or anyone else I'd come across, there was something about her physical presence that I nearly worshipped. I couldn't explain it any more than I could explain any number of the world's wonders, but the grace of her movements, the gaiety of her voice, the beauty of her form, the loveliness of her smile, insofar as the facial scarring allowed – these were as marvelous to me now as when I'd first encountered them. She, on the other hand, had evolved in her response to me. Her initial revulsion, tempered even then by the generosity of her manner, had given way to an acquired comfort, and to displays of gentleness that approached affection. The feel of her hand in mine, even the fleeting touch of it on my shoulder when she passed behind me as I sat; these were as nourishing to me as the very food I ate.

Most evenings, as early as the darkness could effect our conceal-ment, we'd be off in "our chariot," as Margaret called it. We abstained only in extremely wet weather, or after long workdays for the mares. We drove to the west; we drove to the east; we drove up side roads. I learned the abilities of the team, and they to trust in me; and I gauged the limits of the curricle – a tippy carriage by its nature – with increas-ing confidence. Margaret couldn't get enough of those rides; the more I saw her revel in them, the more Saville's long refusals matched his other more obvious cruelties.

She was ever wary of visitors, expecting the knock of constables with every new day, and dreading the havoc they threatened to wreak on our lives. At her continued insistence, I dared not linger in front of the house during daylight hours, and was ever alert for the bell-gate. And we were extremely careful to conceal what clothing I didn't hap-pen to be wearing. Everything else, upon inspection, could be passed off as Saville's – the toothbrush, the foodstuffs, the scent in the sheets. But as Walton had found, clothing cut for an eight-footer had a certain evidential authority. While, in her own words, "dreadfully wanting for fabrics," Margaret had fashioned me some better fitting work clothes; when I wore those, my tailored set was folded into a box and stashed up into the roofboards. When I wore the tailored set, typically in the evenings, we stashed my workwear.

For many weeks we had only quiet. And then, as these things seem to go, we had two visits in a single day. The first occurred at mid-morning, just before tea. The ring of the bell-gate sent me scurrying for cover, though well within earshot.

"Mrs Saville, I presume?"

"Yes, how may I help you?"

"I'm Matthew Broadman, a business associate of your husband's. Is he at home, per chance?"

"No, as misfortune would have it, he's away on business."

"Has he mentioned my name in that regard?"

"No, I'm sorry, Mr Broadman. He doesn't discuss his business affairs with me."

"I haven't heard from him in some time. May I inquire as to when you might expect him?"

"I never expect him, Mr Broadman. He comes and goes as he pleases, often with absences of some duration. I dare say I'm not so different from a sea captain's wife in that regard. If you'd like to leave a card, I'll be sure that he receives it."

The exchange was quickly concluded, the door latched shut, and the horse and rider departed. Exceedingly light fare, it seemed to me, given the dread we'd assigned to it. But Margaret would have no part of my complacency.

"If he'd taken a look about the farm, as a constable might well do, I'd have been hard-pressed to explain the freshly worked fields. Or the ever-expanding paddock."

"Saville must come and go as we require."

"That occurs to me as well. In point of fact, I now expect him as early as this afternoon." We exchanged something like a smile – perhaps more of a grimace on my part, though happily enough intended. "When he's finished his work in the paddock we'll send him right back on his way."

CHAPTER XI

While we'd joked about a second visitor in the spectral person of Saville, the arrival at mid-afternoon was very much real. I was sinking posts when the ring of the bell brought me running for another concealed observation.

"Brother Robert, what a pleasant surprise!"

"My dear sister," he cried, folding her into his arms. "What a joy to see you!"

Overcome with their happiness and my own, I bounded from my perch. Walton turned to me in shock, the same expression I'd seen on many an unsuspecting peasant.

"Franz! How is it that you are here?" He turned again to Margaret. "Has he hidden with you these many weeks?"

"He has."

"Saville, of course, will disapprove, and violently so. What are your plans upon his return?"

"I expect no return."

"Why is that? Where is he?"

"Dead."

"Dead! When? And how? By your hand, Franz?"

"He's dead these many weeks. Franz was only defending me, Robert. Something you might have done some time ago."

"My God. When does the killing stop, Franz? The situation grows increasingly untenable."

"For Franz, or for you?"

"For all of us, Margaret. They'll jail you, as they did me, if you're found to harbour him."

"A short stint in captivity is as nothing to what awaits him. They'll hang him, Robert, and you'll have been the one to bring them."

"I've not been followed, if that's what you mean."

"Nor, in your view, were you being watched before they finally detained you."

"Is Saville's death known to anyone?"

"Only to we three. When asked, I know nothing of it myself."

"And who, pray tell, has asked to date?"

"A business associate named Broadman called just this morning."

"I imagine you'll have more forceful enquiries in the future."

"Because you've led them here?"

Again, Walton declined to answer. He looked at me as if for the first time. I had yet to say a word.

"So you followed the coach, did you?"

"I did."

"And you lost no time in slaughtering Saville. And now you sit in his chair, and eat at his table, and sleep in his bed?"

"I came here with no intent to kill."

"Just as you hadn't intended to kill those men in the lane. But you had every intention of killing Frankenstein's bride. And his dear friend, Clerval. And his dear young brother."

It was Margaret's turn to look at me in shock. We'd never actually discussed those people.

"The dear young brother was not planned," I said.

Now, as if directed in a play, we all took seats without a word or gesture. No one spoke for a full minute, while Robert and Margaret came to terms with what they'd just learned, and I with what Margaret had just learned.

"You never mentioned any killing in your letters, Robert. You were apparently quite happy to arrange my corresponding with a multiple murderer, under completely false pretenses."

"I didn't know you had him in mind for a husband!"

"He's not my husband!"

"Your living arrangements would suggest otherwise."

"Rest assured, we've not engaged in copulation," I said.

"For the love of God," said Walton.

"And what about your manuscript?" she asked, impressively undeterred. "I don't suppose there's mention of any killings in there either. Some man of science you are. Sounds like the publishers were right to pass. And this scientific community you said would protect him – what's come of that?"

"It's most likely to be found in Edinburgh."

"Of course."

"And it occurs to me now that I have in my possession not only a coach, but, beyond all expectations, Franz himself. I might propose we head north very shortly, to drop in on a few natural philosophers."

"You can't just traipse into Edinburgh with an eight-foot murdering monster in tow." Now it was my turn to look at Margaret in shock. "Even if you travel by night, where will you find day lodging to conceal him? How do you propose to 'drop in' on these people? Wasn't that your approach to Pomeranz? How did that work out? Does Franz even like this plan?"

"No, I would far sooner stay here," I said evenly enough, though nursing the wound of her comment.

"Why, so you can strangle me in my sleep? You monster." There it was again! "How dare you pose as the victim after killing all those people? How dare you accept my kindnesses?"

"Your kindnesses?"

"Yes, Robert, my kindnesses. Meals, laundry, housing."

"I see. Well if it's only that, I'm sure Saville killed a lot more people than Franz ever did."

"Faint praise, that."

"And I love what he's done to the exterior. The exposed stone looks fabulous. That was Franz, right?"

"Yes, that was Franz."

I couldn't help but interject. "Did you happen to bring the clothing I left at your place?"

"No, Franz. I had no idea you were here. You might have written."

"We assumed the authorities were reading your mail," said Margaret. "It was the only prudent approach."

"Is that meant to explain the long series of lies you sent me?"

"Misrepresentations, Robert. And yes, with any insight whatsoever, you would see that it explains them entirely. And if you suspected nothing of Franz's concealment here, why haven't you visited these many months?"

"For several weeks I sat at home, waiting for Franz, or for any word from him." He gave me a sour look before returning his attentions to Margaret. "And then I was off to Paris, where a friend made my introduction to two men of science."

"What came of that?"

"I tried something different. I told them the story while we sat for a meal, and I worked them through the lab notes. They gave each other a number of wry looks, and in the end all but declared it a hoax, with all due respect, of course, and with the requisite bows and best wishes on my departure. Not enough detail on the elixir, apparently, to convince them, at least without Franz in tow."

"Just as well, in my mind. And, honoured as I suppose I should be to see you, why not the courtesy of a note to announce your visit?"

"I'd intended to return to London, but a packet happened to be sailing for Bristol, and I took passage on a late impulse. Once in Bristol, I was certain to arrive here before any note. My apologies, sister. I was unaware that we stood on terms of such formality."

Chapter XII

Beyond issuing the occasional command in a terse and dismissive manner, Margaret didn't speak to me for the next four days. Neither her hand, nor the blue of her eye, would suffer to meet mine; nor did she continue her usual practice of accompanying me outdoors for some portion of my labours. But there was solace to be had in her not sending me back to the forest. Not only did I remain under her roof, I held my claim to Saville's room. My privileges there were not expressly confirmed, but nor were they expressly revoked; and when at bedtime I chose to slink up the stairs rather than to slink out of doors, I received no countermanding instruction. Walton slept where he'd slept in the past, in the third bedroom, a cheerless affair with a northern exposure. He was in only slightly better favour with Margaret than I, and, partly as a result of that, gravitated with me to the grounds during daylight hours. I'd not seen him in such a pastoral setting, and found it suited him well. His stride showed a spirit sorely lacking either at sea or in his sunless London abode; he was more naturally outgoing; and any chore appeared to him a pleasure. He happily appropriated all milking duties, and showed a natural facility with all the animals. Beyond his enthusiasm for my having cleared the overgrowth, he took great interest in our fledgling crops, and in the other various projects I'd undertaken. We pruned together in the orchard, cleared in the hayfield, and fenced in the paddock. With his help, progress at the latter was particularly accelerated, to the point that on the fourth day we could pronounce the expansion complete.

Our celebration of that event seemed to lift the cloud off of Margaret. I toured her in the curricle around the paddock's new diameter, Walton walking alongside us with the half dozen sheep who had taken to following me at their every opportunity. Margaret was lively at dinner, and at its conclusion went so far as to suggest an evening ride. Walton expressed his delight at the prospect, and, as the seat would hold only two, volunteered to ride on the standing platform behind. A quarter of an hour later, I pulled up with the team. He walked Margaret from the house on his arm, in a strangely formal manner that evoked something of the church rituals he'd described for me so long before. He helped her aboard, jumped to the platform, and off we went, his head looming over Margaret's and mine, his hands gripping at either side of us.

"A pair of spirited ponies, Franz. You handle them well."

"They do much better with Franz than they ever did with Saville," said Margaret. "He was cruel with them, and you could see their distaste for him in everything they did. Not that I ever saw them from this vantage point."

"They're simply more adept at concealing their distaste for me," I said.

"On the contrary, Franz, I've watched you with the animals, and they love you like their own. It's Margaret you need to worry about." The joke fell flat. "I see that you still struggle with humour, Franz. Actually, that goes for both of you. But in all seriousness, Franz, with her husband so felicitously dispatched, I have no rival as her most seasoned observer. And believe me, for all her brooding these many days, she takes to you as heartily as do the sheep."

"Just what I need, someone else to equate me with the farm animals. Saville was nothing if not persistent in that regard."

"And with special enthusiasm, as I understand it, while hanging them up for the slaughter."

"Yes, he found those moments particularly irresistible."

"Only a fool like Saville would equate an angel with a barnyard beast," I said, surprising even myself with the comment.

"Whoa, Franz!" said Walton. "An angel?"

Margaret gave my hand a squeeze in the dark.

"I would take back the others," I said, "but I'd sooner have slaughtered Saville than any one of those sheep."

"Hear, hear, my friend," cried Walton. "As to the others, what's done is done, and must be attributed to ignorance, isolation, and despair. As to Saville, I only regret that I didn't manage it myself." Margaret squeezed my hand for a second time.

With that, the grievances in our group seemed mostly aired, and largely forgiven. I gave the horses more run, and we lost ourselves in the rushing silhouettes of blackened trees, and in the roar of hooves and wheels on the road.

Walton remained at Sweetbriar another four days, he and Margaret concerning themselves largely with her ability to access Saville's accounts. After some deliberation, they drafted a letter from the dead man himself. He, regrettably, was detained longer than expected, and wished his wife every convenience in his absence. Walton had duplicated his hand after less study and practice than one might expect – he had a natural skill in that regard – affixing the dead man's signature, and waxing the envelope with his seal. On the third day, he and Margaret drove off in the curricle to deliver the letter to the bank, Walton lending masculine credence to what, apparently, a woman could not have undertaken on her own, and thus settling the affair quite favourably. On that same excursion, Walton arranged his transport to London, and engaged a supplier, with credits duly established, to enable Margaret's ordering a variety of goods through the post in future.

I prepared the evening meal while they were away – turnip and creamed mushroom tarts, and a spring salad mix with soft-boiled eggs and apple vinegar. Walton brought up a bottle from Saville's wine cellar – my first taste since arriving at Sweetbriar – and the overall effect was quite pleasing. Margaret held herself to be pleasantly surprised at the quality of our table.

"You must learn to trust me, Margaret. I've advised you on many occasions of Franz's skills in the kitchen. A bit of wine doesn't seem to make a monster of him, either. And by all appearances, I've not brought the police on my tail, despite your rather rude assurances to the contrary."

"I apologize on all counts, brother Robert."

"A toast to my sister, who, in contrast to all her prior comportment, now summons the courage for the most judicious apologies."

"And a toast to Franz, who proves himself quite capable at anything he undertakes."

At this point, Margaret and Walton exchanged looks, and Walton launched into a speech they'd evidently agreed upon, most likely during their time in the curricle.

"I can see how Sweetbriar suits you," he said, addressing me directly. "And, to my great surprise, I see that it suits Margaret, at least under present conditions. More specifically, I can see how your company suits her, and how hers suits you. So, after some deliberation, I've decided to defer to you both; I'll be returning to London without pressing either of you to accompany me. Moreover, and to the great detriment of my own diminishing fortunes, I'm abandoning all pursuit of publishers and of learned men – you'll note that I distinguish between the two – in Edinburgh or elsewhere. It's certain by this course that Frankenstein and his work – which, for all of its misfortunate application, we can certainly admit was brilliant – will fade into obscurity. And it's equally certain that this new course entails ongoing risk for you, Franz; if you're discovered here, there'll be nothing I or anyone else can do for you."

"I thank you for all you've done already."

"On the other hand, we've learned, at some not insubstantial pains to ourselves, that my original course holds no certain salvation on its own account. And if I may be so bold, even a complete success there would hold little prospect of matching the freedom and serenity I see for you here. As for Margaret, while the mysterious disappearance and presumed death of her husband would seem to have opened her path to a more cosmopolitan life in London, I fear that dream is not to be. If I had any hope of its being accepted, I would certainly offer her a home with me."

"And leave Sweetbriar, the place of my most felicitous memories, in the hands of my husband's usurper?"

"The injustice, I'll grant you, would be difficult to overlook. Fortunately, your husband's general surliness and seemingly universal unpopularity should work in favour of Franz's concealment; I wouldn't think there'd be many social calls to contend with. Meanwhile, Franz, I'll post you the manuscript. Destroy it or keep it as you like. It will serve only as a torment and a temptation to me, and the account is rightfully yours."

"And what of the lab notes? I would have them destroyed as the more pressing concern."

"Please pass the salad, Margaret. What a wonderful collection of foraged greens."

"True enough, but an ill-attempted evasion nonetheless," she replied. "Please be so kind as to answer the question."

"I can give no assurance regarding the notes, Franz, except to say that the authorities enjoyed full access to them and did not, to my knowledge, entertain the notion of creating another of your kind, but rather returned them to me with no indication of interest. They are rightfully mine, as Frankenstein's most trusted confidant."

"Nonsense," said Margaret.

"And in my view they retain a certain financial potential, which I would pursue only in the event of your early and unfortunate demise, so as not to procure your living censure."

"You would capitalize on my early demise?"

"Yes, and shamelessly so, as I have not on your living form."

"Frankenstein himself would have had them destroyed."

"As he would have had you destroyed. Even a man as brilliant as he is not to be followed to the letter."

Chapter XIII

A week after Walton's departure, we took delivery of two crates posted from a borough familiar to neither of us. One held many lengths of fabric for Margaret, with the remaining items of my own wardrobe folded within them. Only two pieces were absent, those the constables had seized during their search, the return of which Walton had not dared pursue. The other crate, which the carriage driver vilified bitterly on account of its excessive weight, held two great stacks of papers. These comprised Walton's jumbled manuscript, much of it in my own hand, and an accompanying letter in Walton's.

To Mrs Saville

April 10th, 17—

My Dear Sister:

I am returned to London without incident.

Please accept my sincere gratitude for the hospitality extended during my recent stay. As always, it was my great delight to see you, and to enjoy the many charms of Sweetbriar, which to my eyes has never looked better! I look forward to your reciprocal visit to London, in hopes that it will occur at your earliest convenience!

As mentioned, I was disappointed to see so little of Captain Saville; it seems he is rarely at home during this period, his affairs are so wont to call him away.

Such, I understand, is the nature of his particular business, but it does seem a dear price to pay for you both, given the conjugal harmony you display so commendably in your natural state of togetherness. Please convey him my warmest regards in your next communication.

Your affectionate brother,

Robert Walton

"It is kind of Robert to enquire of Captain Saville," said Margaret.

"He is impeccably considerate. I would expect nothing less."

"Has he included the lab notes?"

"It would appear not," I said. The notes had occupied a different type of paper, written in Frankenstein's peculiar script and very much worn with age and hard use; I could see at a glance they'd been omitted. This was as Walton had indicated, but I couldn't help but feel a certain disappointment, so contrary to Frankenstein's wishes, and my own, was his retention of that material.

While I had little use for the manuscript, and less interest in sorting through it, Margaret's wish to read the original telling set me to the task. But with so many pages destroyed or inked over, reassembling a coherent script proved all but impossible. I eliminated what I could of Walton's retelling, and restored what I could of Frankenstein's original. At Margaret's request, given the state of the pages and my own questionable penmanship, I read it aloud over the course of several nights, filling the many gaps with narrations from my own recollection of the original. These, of course, had been strongly imprinted from my first reading on the ship, and further strengthened over the weeks of painstaking review and futile revision in Walton's parlour. In that way was Margaret more thoroughly apprised of my creator's history, and brought to a fuller reconciliation with my sequential strangling of his loved ones.

We turned the final page on the fourth night. Margaret sat back and sighed.

"I think I'll bathe now, Franz, and wash that unseemly tale from my person. Our histories don't determine our present, or our future. And all scientific genius aside, my brother's regard for Frankenstein is utterly incomprehensible. The man was heartless, irresponsible, and unfaithful. By his attempted reinvention, Robert seems to admit this himself. Chasing you to the pole to make his kind amends, indeed. Would you be so kind as to heat the water?"

This I did, stoking the fire and setting the pots while she made her preparations in another room. She emerged in her robe and boots, and took the seat near the tub. When I'd poured the pots and judged the bath ready, I summoned my courage and knelt unbidden to remove the boots. She said not a word during this process. I stood then to put more pots on the fire, prolonging the task to allow her to enter the tub unobserved. But I heard nothing for such a time that at last I was forced to turn; it was precisely then that she stood, looked me full in the eye, and slipped off her robe. I abandoned our eye contact almost immediately, startled as I was on so many points; the act of her revealing herself; the composure with which she did so; the grace of her movements as she entered the tub; and the holy grail of her form, which, while plainly revealed, caused such bedlam in my brain that I could no sooner process the sight than look directly into the sun. I turned away, and, to justify the movement, began to reset the pots in a clanking, awkward manner. When I turned again, she held my eye once more, this time as she strove to wash her back, lifting her chin, arching her back, and stretching one arm over her shoulder. This sequence had the effect of placing her long pale throat and stunning chest into an indelible focus. I had no choice but to observe these, in a panting silence, through some course of her ablutions.

A word here concerning Margaret's chest: Having been denied the wonder of a mother's milk, I understood full well my particular susceptibility to that adornment of the womanly form. For surely no man born of woman could find himself under such a spell as I and carry on with the work of the world, the building of the majestic cathedrals, the sailing of the great ships, the engineering of the colossal cities, all of which I had seen in but tiny samples during my short time on Earth. But no sooner had I harboured this thought than I'd banished it from my mind. For it was Margaret herself, her particular angelic form, that held the uncommon wonder; my own vulnerabilities notwithstanding, surely she would captivate, if not utterly enslave, any man spared the perversities of Saville, that most justly slain daemon. Only now did I understand the nature of clothing as a requirement of functional society.

At last my better manner took hold; I pulled the chair directly behind her, took the cloth from her hand and made to wash her back myself, running the cloth across her flesh while she held her hair clear. I found special fascination in watching the water run between the candlelit blades of her shoulder, and took the liberty of wringing the cloth to enable and prolong that, drop by tantalizing drop. Increasingly aware that I could no longer justify this activity in the name of cleanliness, I dropped the cloth with the intention of desisting entirely; but on some impulse entirely unforeseen, I wrapped both hands around her neck instead. She stiffened for a moment, as did I. But at that critical juncture I forced my thumbs into a kneading motion, digging gently but insistently into the meat of her shoulder, as I'd done at the hips of my dogs and the chests of the bays. She moaned in what I took to be pleasure, and I continued for some time, running my thumbs on each side of her spine and under each blade. The pots by now exuded large quantities of steam; I arose with some difficulty, and, as Walton and I had done for each other, and she had done for me, poured them into her tub. She gasped at the infusion of heat; but I, who had managed only half-breaths in the last many minutes, found equanimity in this more common courtesy, and once again took the full measure of my lungs.

Chapter XIV

They arrived at our most vulnerable hour, during the afternoon tea. Numbed by the sun on a glorious spring day, and wearied by our labours, our vigilance was then at its low point; and the table set for two would be a most unfavourable discovery. There was no ring of the bell; they'd had the foresight, and the insolence, to stifle the clapper. Worse yet, one man circled the house while the other knocked at the door; I caught sight of him just before he turned the corner, and lay immediately on the floor, holding there until he'd passed back around to the front. Margaret motioned to the tea cups, and I set one of them into the washing basin before slipping noiselessly out the back to crouch near the shed. With the casements swung open, I could plainly hear the conversation at the door.

"Mrs Saville, I presume."

"Yes, how can I help you?"

"Is your husband at home?"

"No, he is away on business."

"Inspector Burke and I are former members of the London Constabulary, currently employed in private investigative work. We don't mean to alarm you, but we've had reports of a fugitive criminal hiding away in this area. We'd like to have a look around your estate for any sign of him."

"Excuse my ignorance, but why would the matter of a fugitive criminal be in the hands of a private firm?"

"It comes down to issues of jurisdiction, madam."

"Meaning the crime was committed at some distance from here."

"Precisely."

"Might I enquire as to its nature?"

"Again, we don't mean to alarm you, madam."

"I appreciate that. But if there's a chance of there being a criminal on my property, I should know the nature of the threat."

"Two murders and a criminal trespass, madam."

"I see."

"Would you mind if we had a look inside the house before we head onto the grounds?"

"What business could you possibly have in my house?"

"On what grounds would you object, Mrs Saville?"

I didn't stay to hear any more, but the ensuing inspection gave me plenty of time to conceal myself beneath a pile of pruned branches in the orchard. I'd have killed them for their impudence, but Margaret would have been gravely displeased; and even I knew that, barring their return, there'd be far more of them to follow. I watched as the men emerged from the house to inspect the shed, and, leaving their bags and jackets just beside it, disappeared down the path to the stables. And I watched as Margaret limped out behind them, went through their bags, removed one particular piece of paper and tucked it into the folds of her dress. She would read it to me just afterwards.

The Worshipful Company of Stationers

Ave Maria Lane

London

April 15th, 17—

My Dear Inspector Collins:

Regarding the murders in Drury Lane, the firm of Booker & Burke has concluded its research on Mr Walton. He appears to be a man of little intimacy and few acquaintants; he does however correspond with a sister, his only living family member and only known confidante, and has recently concluded a stay of just over a week at her home. Her name is Mrs Charles Edwin Saville; she resides with her husband, a retired army officer, on a rural estate in West —.

I believe it is in the public's best interest to rule out this domicile as the sanctuary of the suspect. Given the confidentiality assigned to this case, and the territorial limits of both your budget and your jurisdiction, I propose to further engage the services of Booker & Burke, once again at my personal expense, to make an unannounced visit to that estate. The suspect's highly aberrant physical appearance should make his identification obvious, should he be in residence there.

Failing the receipt of any particular objection on your part by the 20th of this month, I will proceed accordingly. Rest assured that all discretion will be observed.

Sincerely,

George C. Pomeranz

The men passed through the orchard and into the paddock. I moved directly to the wood, where they were certain to go next, and where I would have the clear advantage of them. I'd spent much of my life hiding from men in the wilderness – often large parties of men with hunting dogs – and these were but two Londoners proceeding on their own. Their want of dogs made them particularly easy game; I let them pass, and followed them, unseen, unheard, and unsmelt. They were working through to the canal, which they'd undoubtedly marked from the road. In short order they came to the gravesite, and, after a short, animated conversation, one of them walked back to the shed for a shovel.

I had a long look at the man who waited at the grave. He had a certain stoutness of jaw that I didn't like; for as little time as I'd had to observe Saville in his animate state, this man had something of his manner. But then again, perhaps he had something of every man, muddling his way through an uninspired life. I gave him some credit for animal instinct; he seemed more uneasy than I might have expected, as if aware of being watched by his physical superior. At one point he stared straight at my position; perhaps I'd ventured too close, overly curious about the condition of the dogs I'd heaved in, one atop the other, some months before. But I held perfectly still, certain he couldn't make me out through the brush with the sun low behind me.

I rather enjoyed watching them dig up the grave, taking their turns at soiling their overly dignified clothes, and coming at last upon the dogs. They tossed them out in tandem, one clasping the back legs, one the front. When they climbed out themselves, they were quick to press handkerchiefs to their noses. I wondered at the need for that; the soil seemed to have worked marvels for the corpses, which seemed tidy enough after what I'd seen of Saville. The men inspected them quite thoroughly; I could only envy them from where I sat but resisted all temptation to move closer. After digging enough about the grave to conclude there was nothing more to be found, they kicked the dogs back into the grave with what I thought an unseemly lack of respect, and the soil in after them.

They seemed a bit humbled, in their begrimed and empty-handed state, as they knocked once again on Margaret's door.

"You're aware, madam, that two large dogs are buried along the canal. Fairly recently, I would say, some time in the last few months."

"I've never seen the graves. I can't walk nearly that far, nor would I have any interest in doing so. But my husband told me he'd put them down."

"And why was that?"

"Why was what?"

"Why did he put them down?"

"They were growing wilder and less obedient with age. When they finally killed a sheep, that was the end of them."

"How, might I ask, did your husband kill them? We saw no signs of gunshots."

"I have no idea. But my husband is very good at killing things. I imagine it was quite efficient."

"A military man, is he?"

"Yes, but what of your search? Surely you haven't come all this way to remind me of my dead dogs."

"No, madam, we haven't. And you've nothing to worry about. We've found no sign of the fugitive. Please forgive the intrusion."

With a pair of quick bows they were back through the gate, which rang out clearly on this pass, onto their horses, and gone.

Chapter XV

Walton's visits were regular, and always most welcome. He continued to enjoy the outdoors, regardless of weather, and often set his visits for those times when the work was most robust. Taking in the hay was a great favourite of his; he swung the scythe with a gusto and a grace I couldn't match, even when we'd fashioned an especially long-handled scythe to account for my height. He commissioned the manufacture of a replacement casement for the one I'd smashed, and he and I made the installation, restoring full light to Sweetbriar's best sitting room, and bringing that face of the house to the standards of the others. We built the stone wall I'd envisioned, a handsome run that brought out the contours in the land as if in some painted landscape. And when Saville's skeleton lay thus revealed, we buried it with his dogs.

Beyond the workings of the house and farm, Walton took a new interest in his sister. She expressed her desire to shoot Saville's musket and pistol; and rather than dismiss this as the lark of a half-lame woman, he provided earnest and even-handed instruction, and followed afterwards by putting her in plentiful supply of balls and powder. To Margaret's credit, she practiced with those weapons like other women are said to labour at the pianoforte. In time she could load both in a matter of seconds; and reliably hit a small target at twenty paces with the pistol, and at forty with the musket. It was a point of great joviality when Walton returned after some months' absence, and she outshot him soundly with both implements.

Her other surprising new passion was for mathematics. She had only rudimentary skills in arithmetic, but these were quickly sharpened by her meticulous record-keeping of our agricultural output, and her steady calculations of our requirements for hay and projected yields for all our various crops. On winter evenings when we weren't in the carriage, she suffered me to guide her through more advanced techniques until she'd surpassed both Walton and myself in both the quickness of her figures and the scope of her study. Walton kept us in fine supply of books, mathematical, agricultural, and romantic, and our library grew quickly, filling two standing shelves I built in duplication of the one Margaret already had. In return, we customarily sent him home not only with vegetables and fruit, but with a sheep or two he'd deliver directly to his butcher. Both Margaret and I had reservations at the arrangement, not from any lack of affection for her brother, but from our natural affection for the sheep. But we had such an overabundance of them as to overrun our paddock and decimate our supply of winter feed; and Walton was so generous in his labours and so effusive in his praise of our little farm, that we couldn't help but to share its bounty.

"I remember telling you, Franz, how nothing would grow at gloomy old Sweetbriar, but I could not have been more wrong. You two have done wonders here."

After the visit when his sister had so thoroughly outshot him, we had another parcel from an unknown borough. It held the lab notes, with a letter atop them.

To Mrs Saville

September 29th, 17—

My Dear Sister:

I rather doubt you'd believe me if I simply reported that the lab notes had been destroyed; I therefore post them directly to you, at great pain to myself.

And thus do I wash my own hands of them and assign their fate irrevocably to yours. May this be the final step in conquering the delusions that haunted me in the wake of my final voyage, that which tormented me with a mutinous crew, a ruined mission, a dying dear friend, and a deathly stint between pincer-like walls of ice in the far northern sea. I hope to speak no more of those times, nor to revisit those dreams and delusions that gripped me as firmly as did the ice my ship, and doomed me to mad scrawling for such a period thereafter.

Much as my own station is changed for the better, it is yours I envy most, blessed as you are with your providentially delivered mate, a goodly creature not at all of this world; and settled together on your slice of natural paradise, away from the filth and commotion and the poverty and profligacy of London. He is equally blessed to have such a mate as you, after such arduous journey and against such poorly laid odds.

Your affectionate brother,

Robert Walton

"A strange letter," she said. "It's apparently written for the authorities, should they still hold an interest. And I would give him credit for that, but the references to my mate and his arduous journey are so grossly transparent, 'a goodly creature not at all of this world' so entirely laughable with regard to Saville, that anyone with any familiarity with me would surely know the game."

"Few of us can claim such familiarity, Margaret."

"Through no fault of my own, though at this point I'd have it no other way."

"Consider that it was written not for the authorities, but for you. Clearly Robert had come to some sort of resolution in order to part with the lab notes."

"Tell me Franz, do you consider me 'blessed with a providentially delivered mate?'"

"I consider only myself so."

"You underestimate yourself, and the serenity you've brought to Sweetbriar."

I had no answer beyond a swelling in my chest and a running of the milky fluid.

"If, however, you consider yourself bountifully provided," she continued, "if you've no further need for the creation of a mate, no need to that end for the bones of the charnel-houses or the unhallowed materials of the grave, no need to animate the lifeless clay" – here she paused with a piercing look into my very soul – "then I suppose we are at liberty to honour Frankenstein's wishes. That is to say, to destroy his notes."

"Your thoughts are as mine," I said without hesitation. "Tonight we put them to the torch."

"Though I never understood why, if he felt so strongly, he didn't do it himself."

"I've wondered it myself. Even in a weakened condition, he might have dropped them from Walton's cabin window into the sea. Or, at the very end, ordered your brother to do the same."

"Consigning one's genius to oblivion – it must be more difficult than we can imagine."

"There's some life in me yet, Margaret."

She responded with a laugh, the finest sound in all nature.

Orchard prunings formed the evening's pyre. It was modest in scale, nothing like the inferno that had consumed Saville's ruined flesh. But the prunings had lain to dry for most of the summer and proved pleasingly combustible in their own right; and the night was clear and starry as that one had been; and Margaret and I were once again adorned in our finest attire. I'd built the pyre at the edge of the orchard, and Margaret insisted on arriving by foot. We made our way slowly, moving arm in arm along the same path, now obscured, that Saville had once plowed with his iron cravat.

To me lay the honour of the light; the pyre kindled and flamed. We sat on a great log Walton and I had planed smooth just a week before. The lab notes lay stacked between us. We sat for some time, saying little, before I plucked up the top sheet, crumpled it, and tossed it in the forward bit of the fire, a shallow bed of new coals. We watched it burn and rise away in fiery bits. "'How now, wit! Whither wander you?'" It was a throwaway passage from our prior night's reading, bursting out now unbidden.

"Well said," Margaret answered. "'That was laid on with a trowel.'" She crumpled the next sheet and tossed that in. I took the next, and she the next, crumbling and tossing in turn until, after some minutes, all were silently consumed. I ventured a turn to view her face in profile. I admired its form; it seethed with the glow of the living flame. Daemonic, I first thought it; but then of a sudden it struck me quite differently, as that of an angel warrior, flush with great victory. Her eyes met mine, and she shifted into the empty space between us.

Chapter XVI

Beyond Walton, Mr Garvey the postman, and the occasional driver of a delivery cart, Margaret and I had not a single visitor over the course of three full harvests. We enjoyed good health and a general prevalence of fine spirits and joyful camaraderie between us. We'd had our moments of bickering — I'd even spent a night or two back between the roots of my oak — but in the end we'd emerged all the better. We'd benefited, moreover, from improvements in our farming and preserving techniques, and had successfully introduced a modest wheat crop, which supplied us with flour ample for our purposes. There was little we required from the outside world; and salt, sugar, lamp oil, and the occasional lot of building materials were delivered us as needed and without difficulty. In short, we lived in a private harmony so complete as to fuel the notion that we'd pulled forward some benevolent afterlife. This held especially true for one such as I, whose previous existence had brought such an unbroken string of anguish and despair. Margaret too had endured long hardship, long enough that she retained that small doubt of the skeptic, not as it pertained to my character or companionship, but to the possibility of such a contented life continuing into the untold future. It may surprise you that I would exceed her, or anyone else, in optimism, but one must only consider the duration of our respective miseries. I'd been on this Earth for such a small period of time that three years seemed a convincing case for an alternative and

enduring reality. For Margaret, on the other hand, three years repre-
sented but a fraction of the time she'd suffered, and was insufficient to
convincingly offset it.

In all that time her vigilance had never ceased, and my avoidance
of the front garden during daytime hours was well ingrained. But on a
blustery afternoon in October, as I sharpened tools in the shed, a loud
process that allowed me to hear less than I should, I became aware of
footsteps that were certainly not Margaret's, and were nearly upon me.
I turned to find a man already at the door, staring with a malevolent grin.

"So it's true," he said, and continued to look me over in a remarkably rude manner. He had a large moustache, and a repulsively thick
lower lip, glistening with saliva, that protruded beneath it. He was
ungracefully shaped, wide-hipped and long-armed, and I noted, with as
little expression as I could, a dueling pistol where his jacket hung open
on one hip. I had two choices, to strangle him on the spot, or to invite
him inside for tea so we could learn something of what he was about.
As to the former, pistol or no, he had no idea how quickly I could close
the space between us; I'd have my hands at his throat before he'd even
the thought to reach for it. But the latter would rule by the force of the
one piece of unassailable logic – except by the unlikely circumstance
that he was acting alone, his death would bring many others.

"How might I help you, sir?"

"You already have," he said with an unthinkable smugness.

"May I invite you in for some tea?"

He smiled and gave an overly formal bow. I removed my apron
and led him to the door, where Margaret awaited, fully aware of our
sudden crisis.

"This is Mrs Saville. I am Franz."

He doffed his hat. "My name is Thomas Miller."

"Please take a seat, Mr Miller," said Margaret, with perfect composure. "What brings you to Sweetbriar?"

As he sat, I noticed a matching pistol on the other hip.

"A long quest, Mrs Saville. I've been looking for a man of unnatural appearance, a man whose description seems an uncanny match with what I see here in Franz. Accordingly, I now believe my search is at an end. You would admit he would not be easily mistaken for another man?"

Margaret said nothing.

"Is he employed here?" Mr Miller continued.

"Yes, Franz has been helping with the farm work while my husband is away."

"And yet he is at liberty to invite me in for tea. What do you know of his origins, Mrs Saville?"

"Very little, Mr Miller. But now it's time I knew something of yours. You come onto my property without invitation or the courtesy of a knock, openly flouting a pair of dueling pistols, and I would know your business."

"Suffice it to say, Mrs Saville, that I am a former inspector for the London Constabulary."

"We had two others visit before you."

"Some years ago," he went on, "as part of my professional duties, I reviewed a manuscript taken as evidence from the home of a man named Robert Walton. I believe he is your brother?"

"He is."

"As you are almost certainly aware, he'd been sequestering a man suspected of two murders in Drury Lane, a man not seen these many years since. Your brother's manuscript purported to describe the origins of that man, but the story was so bizarre we had no choice but to dismiss it. We have many hard cases in London, Mrs Saville, and no time for tall tales. Though it had left an impression in my mind – more perhaps than it merited – I gave it little thought until a year and more later, when I happened to visit Geneva. Only then did it re-enter my thoughts. I recalled the name of Frankenstein and the town of Belrive, on the eastern shore of the lake. As the latter lay only a league or so from the city, and as I was more or less at leisure, I hired a carriage for a day trip. There I strolled the shore and had a meal at a scenic little inn, where I struck up conversation with a few of the local gentlemen. They were well acquainted with the Frankenstein family, and with the series of unlikely tragedies that had virtually wiped it from existence – the quickly succeeding and violent deaths of a small boy and his elder brother's new bride; the immediate disappearance of that brother and the subsequent death of Herr Frankenstein himself. A series of odd tales seemed to have grown around this family's misfortunes, silly superstitions by any measure, except for their fitting rather well with the account I recalled from the manuscript.

"My curiosity was so aroused by these developments that I cut short my time in Geneva. Germany was a part of my planned route; I simply accelerated that portion of the trip and proceeded directly to Ingolstadt. At the university there, I secured audiences with Professors Krempe and Waldman, both of whom had instructed the young Frankenstein in the natural sciences. Beyond the admiration of their mutual student for his brilliant intellect and uncommon passion for science, both recalled his odd immersion in the practices of alchemy prior to his entering the university. And both described his later withdrawal into private research, his devotion to which was extraordinary, and his secrecy as to its nature even more so.

"Immediately upon my return to London I ordered the files on the unsolved case. There I found the correspondence between a certain Mr Pomeranz and Inspector Collins, who'd been my supervisor at the time of the murders. It described the hiring of a private firm, Booker and Burke, to investigate Mr Walton in the hopes of tracking the culprit."

"Yes, as I mentioned, and as you presumably saw in the files, Messrs

Booker and Burke made a visit here some years ago. They were good enough to disinter my dead dogs."

"Which is exactly why I took so long to arrive at your door. Booker and Burke are men of my acquaintance, and known to be thorough in their work. But the more time passed, and the more leads led to nothing, the more I began to wonder. Finally, I determined upon my own trip to the country."

"And here we are. I believe you mentioned you'd retired from constabulary work. I assume then that you're not here on official duty, but more likely as a hired agent."

"No madam, I serve no purposes but my own. I am in no one's employ. On the contrary, I've taken great care to conceal my pursuit of this case." Margaret and I exchanged quick glances. "The discovery of a fugitive holds but little interest at this stage of my career, and offers no reward. But the discovery of such a phenomenon as sits here before us, the living blend of alchemy and the natural sciences, is something to which many men would aspire. And very much worth all the time I've invested."

"Please forgive my rudeness, Mr Miller. I'd meant to serve tea."

Margaret retired to the kitchen, and I was left to entertain our guest on my own. He leaned back and clicked the hammers on both pistols.

"You've said very little, monster, but you seem to understand the language. I have some things for you, items left in the files." He opened a satchel and unfurled a long pair of trousers. "Yours, I assume?"

"Yes, and I thank you for returning them."

He threw them on the table and followed with a jacket and a similar comment I can't quite recall, distracted as I was with the next object he pulled from the satchel, my lost pickaxe. He set it heavily on the table in front of him. The longer point was coated to the joint in a residue of black. I couldn't help but reach for it.

"I see this has your attention," he said, pulling it just out of my reach.

"Yes, I'm very fond of that pickaxe. It served me well in difficult times."

His eyes went dark as he pulled one final item, a pair of shackles, from the satchel, and one of the pistols from his hip. "Mrs Saville will apply these to your wrists, and you and I will depart in my coach." From that point his eyes never left mine; nor did mine leave his, though I could hear Margaret in the kitchen, and she wasn't making tea.

"Always consider what's in it for the other man," I said at last.

"What's that you say, monster?"

The blast nearly knocked me off my seat. I'd heard that musket hundreds of times, but never inside the stone box that was our home. It thundered off the walls, rattled off the rafters. The ball smacked through one of Miller's ears and exited through the other. Having sacrificed some speed through the intervening matter, it didn't embed itself in the sideboard, but clacked sharply off it, and rolled dead at my feet. Miller teetered to his left and toppled slowly from his chair; his pistol clacked on the stone and discharged with another roar, this one ripping two inches off the bottom of a table leg. Margaret emerged from the kitchen, accompanied by a cloud of acrid smoke, flushed, and with her chest heaving in a way I very much liked. As she set the musket in the corner, I noticed that gunpowder soot covered the right side of her face; I rather liked that too.

"A fine piece of shooting," I said.

"If I'd shot from forty paces I'd gladly accept your compliments. But at six paces they can only be considered insulting."

"Forgive me."

I handed her my handkerchief, and she dabbed at her face. "I'm afraid I was over-generous with the charge," she smiled. "Shall we proceed with the tea?"

"Yes, I think that we should."

She returned to the kitchen, taking the musket with her. In her absence, I fixed the shackles to Miller's ankles, and a rope to the shackles, and hoisted him over a rafter until he hung quite neatly, upside down, bleeding at something of a torrent into a large ceramic bowl I'd set beneath.

"Nice touch," said Margaret as she re-emerged to set the tea tray.

"I thought you might enjoy it," I answered, leveling the table leg with the dead man's empty satchel.

"Yes, it's lovely. Just like old times." She nudged the body to set it slightly asway, then joined me at table for tea and biscuits.

APPENDIX

Frankenstein is a story bracketed with letters. Only by that device, the letters of Captain Walton fore and aft, could Mary Shelley present the narrative as told by Frankenstein himself, and still deliver its aftermath, the parts immediately preceding and following Frankenstein's death.

Letters in *Daemon* are sprinkled throughout the story. The two appearing in Chapters VII and VIII of Volume I are Walton's rewrites of his unsent originals, those appearing in Shelley's final pages, as he reframes the story of Frankenstein and paints his creature in a more marketable light. These then are a combination of Shelley's text and my own. In order to appropriately attribute Shelley's work, I've reproduced both letters here, with her text in bold italic and my own in plain italic.

M. Reese Kennedy

To Mrs Saville

November 3rd, 17—

My Dear Sister:

I trust you are by now in possession of my correspondence through the 19th of August. A letter so dated, and posted but recently from London, suggests its passage at the courtesy of another vessel we had the rare fortune to encounter in the uncharted waters of the far north. But the truth is altogether more pedestrian; I posted the letter by my own person, both feet firmly planted in the City of

London. *Only now am I at liberty to explain, though the glare of the larger tale will quickly eclipse any interest you may have in the physical journey of its pages.*

The admirable stranger we recovered from the ice fragment — Frankenstein, he allowed, was his name — shared with me, as promised, the fantastical story of his life. The telling occurred in several sessions over several days, and was delivered with the greatest difficulty, owing both to his grave physical condition and the horrors inherent in the tale. I recognized at once the extraordinary nature of the narrative, and committed myself to committing each session to paper immediately upon its conclusion, while my memory was most fresh. The wisdom of this approach was borne out as the story progressed and its scientific significance became more apparent. Frankenstein himself reviewed these notes upon their completion, and took it upon himself to correct and augment them as required.

The full story is a long one and cannot possibly be included within a letter, as I'd originally intended. I cannot spare my own pages, nor risk them to the post; and as they number in the many hundreds, a full week's tedium would be required in writing you a copy. But you'll see it soon enough, I dare say in a handsome leatherbound edition. I feared for a time that I hadn't enough paper aboard the ship; those pages I'd meant to fill with observations and illustrations of natural wonders, I found myself filling with what others would likely view as the ravings of a madman, or, at best, the hallucinations of a solitary and disoriented wanderer. But I have already written to you of the intelligence so evident in his speech, and of the noble nature so readily discerned in his character. In our short time together I'd begun to love him as a brother. You, Margaret, would have taken him to heart, just as I did. And as fantastical as was his tale, I had enough preliminary evidence to suspend the normal disbelief, and enough subsequently to vanquish all doubt.

Frankenstein, from an early age, displayed the most prodigious talents in the sciences. As he freely admitted, however, his youthful interests tended to the discredited pursuits of the alchemists — Cornelius Agrippa, Paracelsus, Albertus Magnus, and the like — who concerned themselves with the transmutation of metals and the search for the elixir of life. As he reached the age for a formalized education

abroad, his professors at the university of Ingolstadt, as could be expected, dismissed such pursuits as ancient and useless drivel, and imposed a rigorous turn to
the more modern pursuits, those branches of science appertaining to natural philosophy. These appeared to him as overly mundane; he rued "**the annihilation
of those visions on which my interest in science was chiefly founded,**"
and having "**to exchange chimeras of boundless grandeur for realities
of little worth.**" But he rose through the academic ranks nonetheless, excelling
particularly in the areas of chemistry and physiology. "**My application was at
first fluctuating and uncertain; it gained strength as I proceeded,
and soon became so ardent and eager, that the stars often disappeared in the lift of morning whilst I was yet engaged in my laboratory. As I applied so closely, it may be easily conceived that my
progress was rapid. My ardour was indeed the astonishment of the
students, and my proficiency that of the masters.**"

"**One of the phenomena which had peculiarly attracted my attention was the structure of the human frame, and, indeed, any
animal endued with life. Whence, I often asked myself, did the
principle of life proceed?**" So deeply did his next words strike me that they
still sounded in my head hours after their utterance: "**It was a bold question, and one which has ever been considered as a mystery; yet with
how many things are we upon the brink of becoming acquainted, if
cowardice or carelessness did not restrain our enquiries.**"

It was two days before he could rouse himself to continue the tale, such were
the ravages of his fever, and, I surmised, his reluctance to continue. Much was
lost to my ear, woefully unscientific in relation to his own; but it seemed that to
understand the elixir of life one needed first to understand its extinguishment. "**I
was led to examine the cause and progress of (bodily) decay, and
forced to spend days and nights in vaults and charnel-houses. My
attention was fixed upon every object the most insupportable to
the delicacy of human feelings. I saw how the fine form of man was
degraded and wasted; I beheld the corruption of death succeed to**

the blooming cheek of life; I saw how the worm inherited the wonders of the eye and brain. I paused, examining and analyzing all
the minutiae of causation, as exemplified in the change from life
to death, and death to life."

His pursuit of nature's secrets was relentless, at the expense of exercise, sunlight, nourishment, and proper rest, and of all the discourse fundamental to the
human condition. This unnatural negation extended over the course of many
months, to the great degradation of his health and of his previously sanguine
outlook. And then, my dear sister, came that part of the narrative which I anticipated in equal measures of excitement and dread:

"From the midst of this darkness a sudden light broke in upon
me – a light so brilliant and wondrous, yet so simple, that while
I became dizzy with the immensity of the prospect which it illustrated, I was surprised, that among so many men of genius who had
directed their enquiries towards the same science, I alone should
be reserved to discover so astonishing a secret. Some miracle might
have produced it, yet the stages of the discovery were distinct and
probable. After incredible labour and fatigue, I succeeded in discovering the cause of generation and life; nay, more, I became myself capable of bestowing animation upon lifeless matter."

Imagine, Margaret, the significance, and the weight, of such a moment!

"When I found so astonishing a power placed within my hands, I
hesitated a long time concerning the manner in which I should employ it. Although I possessed the capacity of bestowing animation,
yet to prepare a frame for the reception of it, with all its intricacies
of fibres, muscles, and veins, still remained a work of inconceivable
difficulty and labour. I doubted at first whether I should attempt
the creation of a being like myself, or one of simpler organization;
but my imagination was too much exalted by my first success to permit me to doubt of my ability to give life to an animal as complex
and wonderful as man. The materials within my command hardly

appeared adequate to so arduous an undertaking; but I doubted not that I should ultimately succeed. As the minuteness of the parts formed a great hindrance to my speed, I resolved contrary to my first intention, to make the being of a gigantic stature; that is to say, about eight feet in height, and proportionally large.

"Who shall conceive the horrors of my secret toil as I dabbled among the unhallowed damps of the grave or tortured the living animal to animate the lifeless clay? I collected bones from charnel-houses and disturbed, with profane fingers, the tremendous secrets of the human frame. The dissecting room and the slaughter-house furnished many of my materials; and often did my human nature turn with loathing from my occupation. Every night I was oppressed by a slow fever, and I became nervous to a most painful degree; the fall of a leaf startled me, and I shunned my fellow-creatures as if I had been guilty of a crime. Sometimes I grew alarmed at the wreck I perceived that I had become; the energy of my purpose alone sustained me: my labours would soon end, and I believed that exercise and amusement would then drive away incipient disease; and I promised myself both of these when my creation should be complete."

You, my dear sister, can certainly guess at the result of these labours. I've already described our sighting of the gargantuan man-figure guiding the first dog-sledge. If that and the chilling delivery of the tale are not enough to confirm its veracity, you'll find more to assure it in tomorrow's letter. I rush this off to make the post, but first I must have your pledge of silence. No one — and in particular your meddlesome husband! — must know of any part of this until a time I judge more favourable than the immediate present. Heaven bless us all.

Your affectionate brother,

Robert Walton

To Mrs Saville

November 4th, 17—

My Dear Sister:

The first week of September found our ship still surrounded by mountains of ice, still in imminent danger of being crushed in their conflict. The cold was excessive. Frankenstein had daily declined in health: a feverish fire still glimmered in his eyes; but his life force was exhausted, and when suddenly roused to any exertion, he speedily returned into torpor.

One morning as I watched his wan countenance – his eyes half closed, his limbs hanging listlessly – I was roused by half a dozen of the sailors, who demanded admission into the cabin. They entered, and their leader addressed me. He and his companions had been chosen by the other sailors to come in deputation to me, to make me a requisition, which, in justice, I could not refuse. We were immured in ice, and should probably never escape; but they feared that if, as was possible, the ice should dissipate and a free passage be opened, I should be rash enough to continue my voyage, and lead them into fresh dangers. They insisted, therefore, that I should engage with a solemn promise, that if the vessel should be freed I would instantly direct my course southwards.

This speech troubled me. I had not despaired; nor had I yet conceived the idea of returning, if set free. Yet could I, in justice, or even in possibility, refuse this demand? I hesitated before I answered; when Frankenstein, who had at first been silent, and, indeed, appeared hardly to have force enough to attend, now roused himself; his eyes sparkled, and his cheeks flushed with momentary vigour. Turning towards the men, he said –

"What do you mean? What do you demand of your captain?

Are you then so easily turned from your design? Did you not call this a glorious expedition? And wherefore was it glorious? Not because the way was smooth and placid as a southern sea, but because it was full of dangers and terror; because at every new incident your fortitude was to be called forth, and your courage exhibited; because danger and death surrounded it, and these you were to brave and overcome. For this was it a glorious, for this was it an honourable undertaking. You were hereafter to be hailed as the benefactors of your species; your names adored, as belonging to brave men who encountered death for honour, and the benefit of mankind. And now, behold, with the first imagination of danger, or, if you will, the first mighty and terrific trial of your courage, you shrink away, and are content to be handed down as men who had not strength enough to endure cold and peril; and so, poor souls, they were chilly and returned to their warm firesides. Why, that requires not this preparation; ye need not have come thus far, and dragged your captain to the shame of a defeat, merely to prove yourself cowards. Oh! be men, or be more than men. Be steady to your purposes, and firm as a rock. This ice is not made of such stuff as your hearts may be; it is mutable, and cannot withstand you, if you say that it shall not. Do not return to your families with the stigma of disgrace marked on your brows. Return as heroes who have fought and conquered, and who know not what it is to turn their backs on the foe."

He spoke this with a voice so modulated to the different feelings expressed in his speech, with an eye so full of lofty design and heroism, that can you wonder that these men were moved? They looked at one another, and were unable to reply. I spoke; I told them to retire, and consider of what had been said: that I would not lead them further north if they strenuously desired the contrary; but that I hoped that, with reflection, their courage would return.

They retired, and I turned towards my friend, but he was sunk in languor, and almost deprived of life.

It is far easier, Margaret, to refuse the man of honour when he lies mute and unseen than when he holds your eye direct. What the men could not stomach in the bright glare of Frankenstein's gaze, they could more easily swallow in his absence. In a sunset encounter on the quarterdeck, they insisted they would not be swayed; and with my gallant champion all but interred below, I consented to the return. **Thus were my hopes dashed by cowardice and indecision.**

September 9th, the ice began to move, and roarings like thunder were heard at a distance, as the islands split and cracked in every direction. We were in the most imminent peril; but, as we could only remain passive, my chief attention was occupied by my most unfortunate guest, who the prior days had been entirely confined to his bed, drifting in and out of the waking world. The ice cracked behind us, and was driven with force towards the north; a breeze sprung from the west, and on the 11th the passage towards the south became perfectly free. When the sailors saw this, and that their return to their native country was apparently assured, a shout of tumultuous joy broke from them, loud and long-continued. Frankenstein, who was dozing, awoke and asked the cause of the tumult. "They shout," I said, "because they will soon return to their homes."

"Do you then really return?"

"Alas! yes; I cannot withstand their demands. I cannot lead them unwillingly to danger, and I must return."

"Do so if you will; but I will not. You may give up your purpose, but mine is assigned to me by Heaven, and I dare not. *I must make amends with this creature. I am weak; but surely the spirits who assist me will endow me with sufficient strength. I have done him grievous harm. Through no fault of his own he is horribly marred; and I have left him without guidance or succor and have abandoned him to the ignorant mobs, at whose hands he has* been harried and beaten, falsely accused of heinous crimes, and banished to the cold and the wilds. He flees me still, despairing of any measure of kindness, from me or from any of our kind. He may yet be noble of character; I must make the intercept before he acts rashly enough to cut his own life short for the fault of others." **Saying this, he endeavoured to spring from the bed, but the exertion was too great for him; he fell back and fainted.**

It was long before he was restored; and I often thought that life was entirely extinct. At length he opened his eyes; he breathed with difficulty, and was unable to speak. The surgeon gave him a composing draught, and ordered us to leave him undisturbed. In the mean time he told me that my friend had certainly not many hours to live.

His sentence was pronounced; and I could only grieve, and be patient. I sat by his bed, watching him; his eyes were closed, and I thought he slept; but presently he called to me in a feeble voice, and bidding me come near, said –

"Alas! the strength I relied upon is gone; I feel that I shall soon die, and he to survive me. During these last days I have been occupied in examining my past conduct; and I judge it thoroughly contemptible. In a fit of prolonged madness I created a rational creature; thereupon I was bound towards him, to assure, as far as was in my power, his happiness and well-being. This was my duty, and in the face of it I fled, as would the lowest of cowards, and hoped to face it no more. Just when the creature was most vulnerable and most impressionable, I shirked my obligation, betraying him and my own honour in the bargain. I was fully justified in not creating a companion for this first creature, even in the face of my solemn promise to do so; but it was entirely my doing that his loneliness and exile made the cause so paramount to his wretched heart.

"Long now have I chased the creature, driven in equal parts by the yearning for my own atonement and for the salvation and reconciliation of that wretched soul. That yearning has been to me as my lash to the dogs. He views me, quite justly, as his betrayer and tormentor, and eludes me at all costs, thinking I bring *him only more of what has come before, or death itself. Alas! to think that he shall carry on to the end ignorant of my true purpose. Think not, Walton, that in the last moments of my existence I harbor any trace of the contempt and disgust I once did for this creature. I feel only compassion, and perhaps some measure of a father's love. The task of his enlightenment was mine, and I have failed as wretchedly as failure will allow.*

"*I would implore you, Captain Walton, to undertake my unfinished work...Yet I cannot ask you to renounce your country and friends to fulfill this task; and now that you are returning to England you will have little chance of meeting with him. But the consideration of these points, and the well balancing of what you may esteem your duties, I leave to you; my judgment and ideas are already disturbed by the near approach of death.*"

His voice became faint as he spoke; and at length, exhausted by his effort, he sunk into silence. About half an hour afterwards he attempted again to speak, but was unable; he pressed my hand feebly, and his eyes closed forever, while the irradiation of a gentle smile passed away from his lips.

That very night, as if Frankenstein had willed it from the place beyond, I encountered this very creature. **I entered the cabin where lay the remains of my ill-fated and admirable friend. Over him hung a form which I cannot find words to describe: – gigantic in stature, and uncouth, his face concealed by long locks of ragged hair. One vast hand was extended, in colour and apparent texture like that of a mummy. When he heard the sounds of my approach, he ceased to utter exclamations of grief and horror, and sprung towards the window. Never did I behold a vision so horrible as his face,** *its ill-favored features distorted all the more for its obvious long-suffering.* **I shut my eyes, involuntarily, and endeavoured to recollect what were my duties with regard to this wretched creature. I called on him to stay.**

I had no plan of action, but only the vaguest sense of purpose. Unbeknownst to my crew, who would most certainly have killed the creature on sight, I harbored him in my cabin as quietly as I could manage, struggling to collect my racing thoughts while fearing not immoderately for my own wellbeing, if not my life. And yet common ground stretched between us; we were both reeling in exhaustion, in fear, and in grief — for in the end he loved his creator as I did. Once his own fears were calmed he made no obnoxious demonstration of his physical superiority. On the contrary, he spoke in the most civilized manner, and even yielded me the first turn on the bed. As we took our respective bouts of long slumber, the seeds were sown for something approaching a mutual understanding. Somewhere between sleep and waking, my own vision for a course of action became clear. I saw the creature as some part gentleman and some part brute; he differed not so much in that regard from most men. But by any reckoning, he comprised a scientific marvel; my solemn duty lay in his safe delivery to the enlightened arms of learned men. The violence of my ignorant crew posed his most immediate threat; my initial instinct to conceal him had been correct, and maintaining his concealment through the balance of the journey was my foremost concern.

From the creature's view, awaking in the relative comfort of my cabin, fed and looked after as the guest of a man who'd not betrayed him to an easily assembled mob, was a revelation in itself. Despite what everything in his wretched past had taught him of the cruelty and treachery of man, he accepted my plan without reservation.

And so we settled into our journey southward, a journey destined otherwise to have been insufferable, my expedition aborted without the slightest scientific contribution, and I the laughing stock of all explorers. Instead, unbeknownst to my most unworthy crew, I shared my cabin with the most significant scientific finding since the debunking of flat Earth.

Through the outlay of some not insubstantial sterling, I prevailed upon the crew, mutinous curs that they be, to deliver us to London, and then to return the ship to Archangel under the guidance of my second-in-command. Such was the creature's natural proclivity to the workings of the sailing ship, that he and I handled that vessel of considerable scale, in exclusion of all other seamen, every night watch for the duration of our journey. I should also mention that though the creature had led a bitter rough life, and all the more so of late, he wasted not a moment of his newfound leisure in idleness, but applied every free waking hour most diligently, to his learning in mathematics and the letters, both of which I oversaw with great satisfaction. Indeed, Margaret, he is nearly my equal in trigonometry; and so far has his writing progressed, I would soon have him compose you a letter!

Upon our arrival at the London docks, he and I alighted under cover of darkness. We made our way through the city on foot, with but one unfortunate incident, the nature of which I shall not relate here. We settled thereupon, and remain still, in my house. Stripped as it is of all staff, we are forced to make our own subsistence; at this we have so far succeeded.

I have taken to calling him Franz. He continues his education while I prepare his and his creator's astonishing story for publication. He has become a great help to me even in that endeavour, functioning quite ably as copy clerk. As I'm sure you've surmised from its unfamiliar script, this very letter is copied by his hand.

The clock strikes 7:00; I must adjourn for the evening meal. It is prepared by the creature himself, and quite competently, if recent history serves as a guide.

Again, Margaret, you must pledge your confidentiality on all of these matters until you have my advice to the contrary. For obvious reasons I am currently unable to travel, but I anticipate with great pleasure our rendezvous at the earliest opportunity.

Your affectionate brother,

Robert Walton

Printed by Amazon Italia Logistica S.r.l.
Torrazza Piemonte (TO), Italy

12384360R00112